Cort look ⸺ ⸺ ⸺ ⸺ chuckle bubbled out of him. "Niera Pascotti, you say the most romantic things in the moonlight. No, I'm not allergic to flowers or anything else. Are you?"

She had once been allergic to emotional involvement, but not anymore. She shook her head.

He lifted the flower necklace over her head. As he draped it over her shoulders, his fingers lingered on her sensitized bare skin.

"This should be perfect," he said softly, his smile supplanted by a serious expression. "It can't slip off, like a single flower. And you don't have to decide whether to wear it on the left or the right."

"It is perfect," she whispered as his eyes held hers in the moon-glow.

"May I have this dance?"

She answered by stepping into the open circle of his arms.

As his hand touched the naked skin of her back, a shiver raced through her, a long-drawn-out quiver that seemed to reverberate through him as he pulled her closer...

Pat Dalton

Pat Dalton has been a full-time writer for fifteen years. Her recent publishing credits encompass fiction, humor, travel articles, and general articles in major national and international magazines. She owns a national business-writing company based in Denver, and is also a literary agent representing several other novelists. Her first foray into print was at the age of ten: a poem in the Denver Post *entitled "Go West." She took her own advice and went farther west herself, making the supreme sacrifice of personally visiting all the Hawaiian locales used in* Twice in a Lifetime, *her first novel for Second Chance at Love. A travel buff "on those rare occasions when time and finances permit," she particularly enjoys incorporating exotic settings into her books.*

Other Second Chance at Love books by
Pat Dalton

Dear Reader:

Drama and sensuality abound in our February releases. *Romantic Times* award-winning author Cait Logan is back with her fourth steamy masterpiece and another larger-than-life, macho-yet-vulnerable hero. And Pat Dalton continues her successful blend of intrigue and romance as she brings lasting love to FBI agent Niera Pascotti, who engaged readers' sympathies as a secondary character in both Pat's previous Second Chance at Love novels, *Twice in a Lifetime* (#368) and *Conspiracy of Hearts* (#406).

A clash of wills ignites tempers — and passion — in *A Lady's Choice* (#432) by Cait Logan. Emily Northrup returns to her hometown to nurse her ailing aunt Sid and finds her already being cared for by the man Emily's vowed to avoid — arrogant yet fascinating Cal McDonald. With matchmaking Sid and all of Methow Valley making bets on the wedding date, how can Emily resist Cal's ardent courtship? Combining folksy humor, rural landscapes, and powerful emotions, *A Lady's Choice* delivers an explosive, wonderfully satisfying romance.

Unlike most of us, Niera Pascotti has no desire to visit the tropical paradise of Tahiti, but she's *ordered* to go by her boss in *Close Scrutiny* (#433). Niera's superiors in the FBI want her to take a vacation while they investigate evidence that seems to incriminate Niera in the murder of her former partner. Her Tahitian holiday throws her into the disturbing company of mysterious, magnetic Cort Tucker. Is Cort her one true love — or a deadly foe? Niera's years of intelligence training are pitted against her heart's deepest instincts in this riveting tale that's sure to please all you readers of romantic suspense and James Bond fans.

Speaking of James Bond, this is a real blockbuster month of thrillers from Berkley. We're publishing *Outbreak*, the latest medical suspense novel by bestselling author Robin Cook; *Moscow Crossing* by another bestselling author, Sean Flannery; *June Mail* by Jean Warmbold, the first novel of a series starring investigative reporter Sarah Calloway; and *Once a Spy* by Robert Footman, which combines espionage and romance. Our larger romance novels include *Devlyn Tremayne* by Aleen Malcolm, set in nineteenth-century Cornwall, which Johanna Lindsey has called "a fascinating story full of wonderful people," and *Peacock in Jeopardy*, set in contemporary India, by award-winning author Katharine Gordon. For Regency fans, we're releasing *The Vir-*

tuous Mistress by Pamela Frazier, aka Ellen Fitzgerald, and reissuing *Sylvester or the Wicked Uncle* by Georgette Heyer. Our Barbara Cartland Camfield novel is *A Caretaker of Love*. For mystery buffs, there's *Soon She Must Die* by Anna Clarke, a real treat available in paperback for the first time; *Thirteen at Dinner* by Agatha Christie; and *A Wreath for Rivera* by Ngaio Marsh. And for those of you who enjoy nonfiction, we recommend *Life Wish*, actress Jill Ireland's inspiring story of her victory over cancer, and *Good-bye, I Love You* by Carol Lynn Pearson, a critically acclaimed love story unlike any other.

Until next month, happy reading!

Sincerely,

Joan Marlow

Joan Marlow, Editor
SECOND CHANCE AT LOVE
The Berkley Publishing Group
200 Madison Avenue
New York, NY 10016

SECOND CHANCE AT LOVE™

PAT DALTON
CLOSE SCRUTINY

BERKLEY BOOKS, NEW YORK

CLOSE SCRUTINY

Copyright © 1988 by Pat Dalton

All rights reserved. No part of this publication may be reproduced or transmitted in any form or by any means, electronic or mechanical, including photocopy, recording, or any information storage and retrieval system, without permission in writing from the publisher.

Requests for permission to make copies of any part of the work should be mailed to: Permissions, Second Chance at Love, The Berkley Publishing Group, 200 Madison Avenue, New York, NY 10016.

First edition published February 1988

ISBN: 0-425-10681-0

"Second Chance at Love" and the butterfly emblem are trademarks belonging to Jove Publications, Inc. The name "BERKLEY" and the "B" logo are trademarks belonging to Berkley Publishing Corporation.

Second Chance at Love books are published by
The Berkley Publishing Group
200 Madison Avenue, New York, NY 10016

Printed in the United States of America

10 9 8 7 6 5 4 3 2 1

To my sister
Marleen Wasson
who never reads my books,
but who at least has never smashed
my word processor.

Special thanks to Sharon Rooney, Cheryl Gregorio, Connie Wright, and the staff of American Hawaii Cruises for their assistance in researching this novel.

Prologue

THE SLIVER OF moon cast a muted platinum luster over the rippling waves of the South Pacific. Like seductive hula dancers, two palm trees swayed gracefully in the breeze. Along the corridors of that same breeze wafted the scent of a thousand tropical blossoms.

Niera Pascotti breathed deeply of the sweet fragrance, then emitted a long sigh. Of such elements, she reflected, romances were spun.

Niera sat up straighter, chiding herself for such an uncharacteristic turn of thought. But she allowed her gray eyes to wander over the profile of Royce Taggart, who was seated beside her, behind the steering wheel of the parked Toyota. His strong features silhouetted against the crescent moon appeared sculptured from dark lava-rock. That image was completed by his umber hair and mustache, and further extended by his black shirt and slacks.

His expression seemed dark, too. She noticed more tension than usual knotting his hard features.

In a lame attempt to keep her mind on business, Niera remarked, "Nice night for a stakeout."

"Nice night for a steak-in afterward." Royce's twin dimples deepened in a smile. Refusing to let her concentrate on business, he reached over and caressed her cheek with the back of one long finger.

She was aware of the blunted ridge of a callus remaining from his last undercover assignment, which had required some heavy physical labor. That activity had only temporarily replaced his regular workouts at the FBI gym. The black shirt he wore clung to and accented the male contours of his broad shoulders and muscled arms. Royce Taggart had a powerful build despite his five-foot nine-inch stature. Niera liked his height; he didn't dwarf her, even though she was only seven-eighths of an inch over five feet tall—if she teased her blond hair to a wee bit more fullness on top.

Royce Taggart was handsomer than any FBI agent should be. Niera had formed that opinion a month ago, when he was temporarily assigned to her home base in Honolulu to follow through with an investigation he'd begun on the Mainland. Her opinion was, of course, a purely professional observation of his ability to remain nondescript in the field; it was not prejudiced by the threat he posed to her emotional equilibrium.

Unaware that he was a menace to her valued independence, he said in his deep voice, "I have champagne chilling in a Styrofoam chest in the back seat. I'd have brought a sterling-silver ice bucket, but I was afraid it would rattle."

It was she who was rattled, Niera realized. But she returned his smile. "Styrofoam notwithstanding, my crystal awaits your champagne."

They were planning to have dinner at her apartment later. She actually owned two fine crystal wineglasses and two place settings of fine china, which she'd purchased twelve years ago—at twenty, Niera had been more eager to impress her male companions. Tonight she had retrieved from the bottom of a dresser drawer the lace tablecloth her aunt had given her, and the Formica top of her kitchen table was now peeking through the delicate pattern. At its center, in a gleaming silver holder, stood a spiral-shaped red candle.

For an instant, Niera likened herself to that candle, standing alone, waiting for the right man to ignite her with a glowing flame. Was Royce Taggart that man? she asked herself for the umpteenth time. She certainly felt attracted to him, more than she had to any other man in recent years. But was that enough?

She hadn't made any decisions yet, although Royce had been hinting that he was ready for the next step in their personal relationship. In addition to the many hours spent together on this investigation, they had dated several times—dinner out, movies, musicals at various community theaters. Last weekend, they'd hiked along the Na Pali Coast on the nearby island of Kauai, spending the night together—but in separate sleeping bags.

Niera silently wondered if she had become so enamored of the idea of heart-spinning, fantasy love that she might not recognize real love if it came along. All her adult life, she had been alone by choice. Never had she been lonely, but recently she had become aware of a void in her life, a subtle but lingering emptiness.

Niera sighed again.

"A set of infrared binoculars for your thoughts," Royce teased. "And I'll throw in a stick of gum, too." He retrieved a pack of licorice-flavored gum from his pocket and offered it to her.

"I guess it is my turn to watch for a while, but I'll pass on the sticky stuff." Royce was the only licorice addict she'd ever met. He was rarely without licorice gum or candy.

As she reached over to take the binoculars from him, he grasped her hand in his.

"Royce!" Her protest sounded more wistful than scolding.

"I don't recall ever reading in the FBI manual that two agents can't hold hands on a stakeout."

"I think it does say something about keeping your eyes on the object of surveillance, though." He was gazing at her instead of at the long rows of warehouses before them.

"Despite the ocean and the moonlight, this isn't exactly the ideal setting for romance, even with scent of frangipani blossoms blowing our direction from that truckload of flowers over there," he admitted.

He grabbed a tissue from a box on the dashboard. "Damn pollen," he managed to say before he sneezed. Royce Taggart was, inconveniently, allergic to paradise. But he claimed to adore living in Honolulu anyway. "They certainly spoil a guy's romantic image."

"It could be worse. You could have chronic hiccups." Niera laughed along with him.

"I love your laugh." Royce's deep voice washed over her. "It reminds me of silver bells."

"Silver bells. Hardly appropriate for a balmy night in Hawaii. Maybe I'd be better suited to a snowy street-corner on Christmas Eve."

"You *are* like Christmas to me," Royce murmured. "Cozy-warm, full of joy and promise, and wrapped up with tasteful elegance."

Niera's usual quick response wouldn't come. She swallowed hard. She hadn't realized the depth of Royce's feelings for her. Maybe she'd been too busy fearing that she'd be the one who cared the most, as she'd been with her first love, Sam Draper. Now suddenly she was concerned that maybe *she* didn't care as much as Royce.

"As I was about to say before the pollens ganged up on me," he continued, "I wish we were alone on a deserted beach, where I could make your silvery eyes sparkle just for me and tell you how the moonlight pales in comparison to your golden hair."

"I didn't know you were so poetic," she murmured. Flattered but somehow uncomfortable, she deflected his words by joking, "Of course, the moon doesn't have much going for it right now." Once again, she glanced toward the pale sliver in the faraway depths of the night sky.

He lifted her hand to his lips.

"Royce," she heard herself saying, "we're still on duty."

"For a little while." His statement was an affectionate warning. "But you're right. We'd better get back to business." He shifted in the seat. "You know, stingy Hal is probably going to deduct the price of my binoculars from my next paycheck. If I hadn't misplaced them, we could both be staring at the same lack of movement."

"Our revered boss is merely guarding the taxpayers' money with his economy measures." Brushing a stray lock of medium-length blond hair back from her tanned cheek, Niera raised her own infrared binoculars toward a warehouse that stood at the seaward end of a wide concrete pier extending far out into the ocean. The weathered wooden structure came into focus along with the other buildings that lined both sides of the pier.

"Do you suppose the taxpayers know that their money is being spent to preserve the integrity of designer labels?" A trace of bitterness etched Royce's words.

"My cousin would be impressed that I'm a guardian of fashion, if only our work wasn't secret," Niera commented lightly. "She would never suspect me of staying on top of clothing trends," she added.

"You always look nice." He sounded sincere.

"Thanks," she replied simply. "But I just wear what I like. I don't follow the fads or the dictates of those designers who introduce some outlandish new look every season to keep the cash flowing into their own pockets." Tonight she was a candidate for the Most Dully Dressed List, wearing jeans and a dark shirt for the stakeout instead of her favorite bright island prints.

"I've never minded checking out the labels on women's jeans," Royce kidded, "as long as there were women inside them."

"A chauvinist pigskin remark. Don't forget that you and I are the first line of defense for men's briefcases. And even for men's briefs."

The United States had been increasingly flooded with bogus merchandise cheaply produced and fraudulently labeled with the names of prestigious designers. Niera and Royce suspected that the criminal ring they were attempting to net had begun as a small operation—a few people assembling clothing with counterfeit designer labels in a couple of basements in Miami. But some of those criminals were masterful entrepreneurs, and their business had boomed.

The operation had spread to several states and then had continued to expand. Now the ring was importing phony merchandise from Asia and Latin America. U.S. Customs had passed all available information along to the FBI. Since the Bureau was responsible for upholding laws governing U.S. trademarks and copyrights, it remained in charge of the case.

Niera had come to suspect that the dilapidated warehouse now under surveillance was probably the primary receiving and distribution point for counterfeit clothing and toys imported from Asia. Now she and Royce were looking for hard evidence to back up that suspicion.

Despite the wry jokes Niera and Royce made about being assigned to such a tame case, brand-name counterfeiting had serious effects that went far beyond stitching on an alligator where it didn't belong. Already on record were helicopter, bus, and car accidents caused by the failure of bogus parts, as well as life-threatening reactions to fake prescription drugs and medical devices.

"While I was watching an old John Wayne movie the other night," Niera said, "I thought how this was sort of twentieth-century rustling with a twist. In the Old West, they altered brands on livestock by changing an N to an M or some such thing. Now we see cheap Bolex become Rolex, and Aseikon become Seiko."

"And the public responds by the thousands to ads that actually offer genuine phonies."

Genuine phonies. She certainly had seen plenty of those. And Niera wasn't thinking merely of products . . .

While they took turns watching through the single pair of binoculars for the next couple of hours, they conversed easily, as always, on a variety of subjects. Maybe this was what being in love was all about, Niera thought—never running out of things to talk about, no matter how often you were stuck together in otherwise boring situations.

"Sorry," Royce said at one point. "I know how you hate it when I smoke in the car, but we've been stuck in here too long. I promise to puff out the window."

He turned the binoculars over to her and reached inside his pockets for cigarettes and matches. Quickly, he lit a mentholated cigarette. For an instant the tiny flame was reflected in his pale blue eyes, creating an image of fire and ice.

"Be careful your mustache doesn't turn into a torch," she teased, to soften her forthcoming firm reminder. "It would have been better to use the car lighter, Royce. A match can be easily seen from a distance."

"You're right. I'll watch that in the future. Or maybe you're the person to reform me. Later, we'll discuss how to motivate me to give up smoking entirely."

She grinned. "You mean, besides better health, longer life, probably fewer allergy problems—"

"Long life sounds good," he said. In the darkness, she could barely make out the wink he aimed in her direction. "But I want to make sure it's worth living."

While she resumed the vigil, Royce popped a cassette into the stereo tape-player, lowered the volume and hummed along with the overture to *West Side Story*. They had discovered in earlier conversations that it was their favorite musical—not only for its beautiful songs but for its centuries-old story of star-crossed, doomed lovers.

Eventually, Royce remarked, "There's a storm coming."

Niera glanced up, handing him the binoculars, since it was his turn. Darkening clouds hovered over the remnant of moon, then engulfed it.

"I'm going out on the pier to take a look around," he said.

"But we don't have a search warrant yet," Niera protested. "And Hal doesn't want us to risk blowing the investigation until we're sure this is the central location for the smuggling operation."

"So I'll see what I can see without a search warrant." Royce didn't meet her gaze.

She was aware that some of her colleagues occasionally stretched the rules in pursuit of justice. The agents usually tried not to let anyone find out about it, and they covered for one another when necessary.

"I don't have to break down the door," he pointed out. "That warehouse is in terrible shape; there are probably loose planks all over the place. I'll bet the local kids go in and out all the time."

"I'll come with you."

"No, you stay here."

She bristled. "Is that a male-chauvinist command?"

"It's a direct order to you from the senior agent on this case, namely me. Wait right here in the car until I get back."

"But—"

"No arguments."

It had been a long time since a male partner had patronized her in the course of an investigation. Or was Royce simply saving her from possible illegal involvement while sparing himself an eyewitness if he planned to expedite the investigation by breaking and entering?

The pier had been deserted and quiet all evening, so Royce's solitary mission probably wouldn't prove to be dangerous. Still, to make her position clear for the future, Niera said, "We'll talk about this when you get back."

"When I get back, it will be time for us to go off duty. And I have other things in mind besides talking about this." He opened the car door.

"Be careful." It was an often-heard comment, made to any partner on any case.

He leaned toward her, suddenly gathering her into his sinewy arms. His lips found hers in the midst of the black night, and he kissed her long and longingly.

He tasted of licorice-flavored smoke. Niera yielded to his urgency, and found herself kissing him back just as hungrily.

But was she ready for more than an occasional kiss? Later tonight, or any night soon?

As he drew away, she traced his mustache with her fingertip.

He got out of the car, then bent down and looked back in at her.

"I love you, Niera," Royce said simply, directly.

He was gone before she could respond.

In fact, she realized, she didn't know how to respond. She wanted to be in love. But . . .

Maybe she'd been overexposed to romance lately. It had seemed to blossom all around her—for everyone except Niera. First she'd been assigned to guard a relocated witness named Lincoln Stanford, a.k.a. Chase Granger, shortly before he was reunited with his true love, Kelly Nyles. Soon thereafter, her good friend, intelligence agent John Eric Trevor Randall, had let his heart run literally away with employment-agency manager Lisa Rollins.

Niera had always been subjected to an onslaught of weddings of friends and co-workers, somewhat tempered by a burgeoning divorce rate among the once-radiant couples. Niera recognized that her recent longing for a love of her own might have been generated by the fact that, years ago, thoughts had flitted through her mind of becoming Mrs. Lincoln Stanford or Mrs. John Randall.

She watched Royce follow an uneven course toward the warehouse, keeping close to the cover of the other buildings, until she had trouble spotting him among the shadows.

In that moment, she realized that she couldn't define Royce Taggart, mentally and emotionally, any better than she could distinguish his physical form from those shadows. Despite the many hours they'd spent together and the long talks they'd had, she wasn't sure she knew the real man. What were his deepest feelings? she wondered. What values did he hold sacred?

She was aware of a lot of facts, she realized. She knew, for example, that Royce was an only child, just as she was. Unlike Niera, however, he had no relatives at all. His mother had died a few years ago; he had no idea where his father was; he didn't even have cousins or aunts and uncles to ease his sense of isolation. But what else did she know about him? Niera asked herself.

And why had he told her so little about himself? Had he been an undercover agent for so long that he'd fallen out of the habit of discussing his thoughts and feelings?

Niera allowed herself a wry smile, admitting silently that she, too, had fallen out of the habit of confiding in others.

She squinted into the darkness at the end of the pier, wishing Royce had left the binoculars in the car. Storm clouds completely covered the moon, making the night so black that she could no longer make out the shape of the warehouse. What if someone else approached the building while Royce was there?

Heedless of the senior agent's official orders, Niera got out of the car and crept toward the warehouse, following much the same route Royce had chosen. From habit, she sought out the darkest shadows as she worked her way toward a better vantage point.

She could keep watch until Royce started back and still return to the car before he did, she assured herself. He'd never know that she'd disobeyed his orders if she chose not to tell him.

She headed onto the pier, treading carefully over the crumbling cement.

Suddenly, a shaft of the moonlight pierced the clouds. Niera sprang into a doorway.

Another dark figure was visible for an instant at the seaward end of the pier, ducking around the corner of the farthest warehouse.

Quickly, Niera drew her gun. It chilled her fingers where so recently she had felt the warmth of Royce's hand.

She had to find the other person immediately, or else find Royce and warn him of this possible new danger.

Rapidly zigzagging from one dark niche to another, she moved forward until she had covered more than half the length of the pier.

An ear-shattering boom split the night. Flashes of white, yellow, and orange shattered the darkness.

Shock waves from the explosion slammed Niera against the concrete.

Royce must be dead.

That knowledge was conveyed to Niera in the whispers of the nurses. In the evasions of the doctor, who had avoided answering her questions about the other patients. In the sobbing of the rain outside her window.

Yet Niera couldn't believe he had died, couldn't accept it, despite the unexplained emptiness gnawing within her, surpassing her other aches and pains.

It was late afternoon. More than two hours had passed since she'd finally struggled up through the blackness that had enveloped her ever since the explosion. The doctor had explained that she'd been unconscious for four days.

But she harbored vague recollections of earlier struggles to come out of the darkness, and she knew there had been brief moments of awareness during those four days. Phantom wisps of memories taunted her. People moving around her room. Doctors and nurses, she supposed. But hadn't there been someone else? A man with a deep voice, whom she associated with a spicy-minty fragrance?

As Niera tried to shift to a more comfortable position in her hospital bed, she felt a stab in her side. That would be the cracked rib the doctor had mentioned. She gently touched the gauze that covered her forehead, forgetting about the tight bandage on her injured wrist. Above that, a plastic tube dripped glucose into a vein in her arm. She glanced at the heavy cast on her left leg, which was in traction.

Flowers bloomed on the dresser and bedside tables. As soon as she'd regained consciousness, Niera had insisted on seeing the cards that had accompanied the flowers, clinging to the hope that one of the arrangements might be from Royce. She had been disappointed.

Now she focused her gaze, along with her last remaining hope, on the only arrangement that didn't have a card. Those bird of paradise blossoms, in hues of blue, orange, and yellow, might be harbingers of a brighter tomorrow. She tried to keep on believing that Royce had sent them.

A nurse entered her room. "Still awake? That's good!" she said with practiced cheerfulness.

Before the door closed, Niera caught a glimpse of a blue-uniformed policeman stationed outside her room.

The nurse plumped the pillows and, at Niera's request, raised the head of the bed slightly.

"I need to know about my partner—" Niera ventured again.

"Your supervisor's on his way to see you now," the nurse interrupted, hurrying out of the room without meeting Niera's eyes.

Her last thread of hope that Royce might be alive was rapidly unraveling.

Niera stared out the second-story window through a sheet of rain at the area within her limited field of vision. Soon a film of unshed tears blurred the scene even more.

Roiling clouds glowered in the sky, their vast gray scowl stretching all the way across the horizon. The storm raged with such intensity that even the Hawaii Visitors Bureau wouldn't dare refer to it as the islands' usual liquid sunshine.

Niera kept staring out the window anyway, as nature gave vent to its fury.

Eventually, a shaft of sunlight forced its way through the clouds. Below her, the vivid flowers, trees, and green grass began to sparkle with diamonds of fresh moisture.

Then she saw him.

He wasn't so far away that she couldn't recognize him immediately. Despite the hooded yellow slicker and the fact that he'd shaved off his mustache, she knew him at once.

Royce!

He was standing motionless, looking up at her window.

Joy and relief made her heart do flip-flops. She tried to signal him, waving her right arm, but she knew he couldn't see her.

Somehow he'd avoided being injured in the explosion. Thank God!

But why was he standing outside in the rain instead of coming to her room?

Probably he'd been here all along, she reasoned, recalling the vague memory of minty after shave. He'd just gone out for a meal or a walk and was on his way back to her room now.

She smiled when his gaze seemed to catch and hold her own. Then her attention was diverted as the door to her room opened.

Her fiftyish and balding supervisor, Hal Symons, entered, damp from his own encounter with the rain.

"Hal, I'm so glad to see you."

He crossed rapidly to her bedside and gave her hand a quick, slight squeeze. "Glad to see you, too, Nip."

"It's been a long time since you used that nickname." Several years ago, the older agents had taken to calling her Nip.

"I still remember how the name came about," Hal reminisced. "We took your initials, Niera Ilene Pascotti, because they described so well your practice of relentlessly nipping at the heels of the bad guys until you herded them into a corner."

"That's right," she said. "And I'll round up the next batch, too, as soon as I get out of here." She continued in a rush, "Hal, it was awful at first. No one would tell me anything about Royce. I'm so relieved now."

"Relieved?"

"To know that Royce is okay."

"Niera," Hal began, with greater formality, "Dr. Chu told me it would be all right to talk to you now."

"Good."

"Did he explain to you that memory problems are common after a concussion?"

"Yes. He said I might not be able to remember things that happened just before the injury occurred, and perhaps even for several days afterward."

"And yet Dr. Chu says your memory seems to be fine."

"It is." When Hal didn't speak immediately, she continued, "That isn't an impossibility, you know. I suppose all my special training helped." She blinked her eyes to battle the sleepiness that had returned since her terrors about Royce's fate had been vanquished.

"Then you know what caused your injuries?" Hal asked hesitantly.

"Of course." He waited for her to continue, so she recited patiently, "There was an explosion at the warehouse on the pier. I must have been knocked down by the shock waves or injured by flying debris, or both."

"And was Royce with you at the time?"

"No. He must have told you that himself. I thought he was inside the warehouse, but thank God he wasn't, or at least he wasn't in the part that blew up."

In a tone that was gentle on the surface but underlaid with cold steel, Hal said, "The explosion was tremendous. There is nothing left at that end of the pier, not even the pier itself."

A fog began to hover around Niera's brain, blotting out the thoughts trying to take shape. "Well, then, Royce must have started back toward the car before the explosion," she murmured, trying to reason her way through the situation. He hadn't had time to complete his search, but maybe something had caused him to turn back. Maybe he, too, had seen the man at the end of the pier.

Hal's voice penetrated the fog. "Niera, we haven't seen Royce since the explosion. We searched the area thoroughly, but the currents around that pier are so strong that—" His voice cracked, and he left the rest of his thoughts unspoken. "Niera, the reason it took me so long to get here today is that I was attending the memorial service for Royce."

Why would there have been a memorial service? Niera wondered. Not comprehending his words, she gestured toward the window. The pain that jabbed her arm was almost a welcome distraction. "Hal," she said almost desperately, "Royce is outside. He's right down there."

Hal stepped to the window and looked out at the hospital grounds.

Niera realized that he saw the same thing she now saw.

A deserted landscape.

The rain had started again, but lightly this time, so that the curtain it threw across the scene was transparent. Nobody was there.

All that awaited outside her window was a sky draped in funereal black, weeping a deluge of tears upon the earth.

The next afternoon, Niera lay in bed, mumbling answers to the fourth-grade-level questions being asked on a TV game show. Television and magazines were the only diversions the doctor would allow.

Hal had left shortly after they'd gazed out at the empty landscape together, and she'd soon been cushioned in a deep sleep that lasted almost twenty-four hours.

Now Hal returned, knocking on her door, then entering the room. A somber expression froze his features.

"The doctor says you're up to answering some questions now," he said by way of greeting.

"Sure. Let's get on with it." Regardless of whether the explosion had been planned or accidental, she wanted the criminals caught without delay. "I left written reports in the office every couple of days. I completed an up-to-the-minute detailed report on the day"—her voice caught momentarily—"just a few hours before the explosion. It's in the files with the others. The only new information I can add is what little I know about that night."

Hal took notes as she related the events that had preceded the explosion.

She omitted only the personal facts. That Royce had said he loved her. That she wished she could have given the response he wanted to hear. That in every waking moment, doubts and questions pummeled her mind and her heart: Could she have done anything that would have saved Royce?

If Royce really was dead. Why did that trace of uncertainty persist in a corner of her mind, confusing her thoughts even more?

Hal said they had reviewed her written reports, and yet he interrogated her over and over, asking the same questions, getting the same answers. *Interrogate* was the right word, Niera thought, for the way Hal was questioning her. But Hal, like any other law-enforcement officer, would be extra eager to catch this ring of counterfeiters, now that the case involved the death of an FBI agent.

"You're sure you have nothing else to tell me?" Hal said finally.

"I wish I did know something that would help, but that's it. Much as I'd like to deal with these crooks myself, I hope you'll have closed in on them before I can be out of this bed."

"Dr. Chu says you can be moved to another hospital in a few days." Hal stood and walked to the window, staring out. "I'm transferring you temporarily to Great Falls, Montana, as soon as he gives his final okay. You'll share a hospital room there with a young woman named Megan Overett, who's a protected witness on a different case. There'll be other FBI agents on guard duty, but you'll provide some extra protection for Megan, and be company for her besides."

"But, Hal," she protested, "guarding protected witnesses is junior-agent stuff!"

"You have to recuperate someplace."

"But I wouldn't be worth much right now in an emergency. And you know how I loathe cold climates. I want to stay here. Maybe I can help some way on the case, even if I can't be up and around yet."

"Don't push it, Niera," Hal said quietly.

"What do you mean?" she asked, feeling suddenly chilled.

He looked her directly in the eye. "Some of our leads indicate that you may be in cahoots with the counterfeiting ring."

Flabbergasted, Niera leaned back into the pillows. "What's the evidence?" she managed to ask.

"You know I can't discuss specifics with you. Obviously, there's no evidence that I consider solid, or you'd be under arrest. I'm taking your past record into consideration, of course. Consider yourself lucky that I'm not placing you on suspension."

These shocking new pieces of information clattered around her mind until a few bits fell into place. She would be under guard and constrained, just like the witness she was supposed to protect. Even her telephone calls and correspondence would automatically be screened.

She knew there was a guard outside the door of her hospital room, but she had assumed he was stationed there for her protection. Now she realized he was also there to keep her supposed criminal cohorts from contacting her. The bedside telephone, she realized, was probably bugged.

"Am I being temporarily shunted to Montana because you believe in me, Hal? Or because you don't want your department to look bad until you're sure I'm guilty?"

"Maybe a little bit of both," he admitted.

The next few days plodded past.

Niera received a long-distance call from the Cayman Islands from her old friend John Eric Trevor Randall. The grapevine had twined that far, and he wanted to know what he could do to help her. She gratefully but firmly refused his help. Only a week before the explosion, she'd flown to Florida at the request of her supervisors to try to talk John out of resigning from the Bureau. But he'd quit anyway, and Niera was happy for him and his fiancée, Lisa Rollins. No way would she ask John to become involved in the world of intrigue again on her behalf.

And she couldn't involve any other friends or contacts in the FBI or other law-enforcement agencies. She presumed the word was out that she was under suspicion and shouldn't have access to the normal channels of assistance. Anyone who helped her now might fall under suspicion, too, and she wouldn't subject her friends and colleagues to that.

She was on her own. Totally.

She reasoned that her best course would be to get herself back into shape, physically and emotionally. Then she could solve this case and prove her own innocence.

On her last afternoon at the Honolulu hospital, the

nurse pushed Niera's wheelchair into the bright sunlight
on the ground-floor lanai, as Niera had requested. She
lifted her face to the warmth, wondering if this would
be her last time in the sun, and not minding if her right
leg became tanned while her cast-encased left leg stayed
pale. She breathed in fresh tropical air, scented by the
varieties of flowers on the landscaped grounds.

She glanced through the assorted magazines available for patients and settled on a travel magazine. On a
page where she was leaving Antarctica and heading toward Madagascar, she dozed off.

She awoke abruptly when the magazine slipped off
her lap and onto the concrete floor. The sun was much
lower in the sky, spinning shadows beneath the trees.

She saw him immediately.

Royce stood nearby in the dusky shade of a poin-
ciana. Her sudden awakening caught him unaware, and
a startled look crossed his features.

"It *is* you." She drew out her words in a combination
of surprise, relief, and puzzlement. Besides shaving off
his mustache, Royce had bleached his hair blond. But
she recognized him easily.

For an instant, he didn't move. Then, an expression
of panic gripped his features, and he pivoted and hurried
in the opposite direction across the grounds, his pace
just short of a run.

"Wait!" Niera called after him. Her tone became
more plaintive. "Please wait."

Releasing the wheelchair brake, she tried to follow.
She bumped over the edge of the concrete lanai, but the
wheels refused to turn rapidly on the damp grass. Her
tone of voice changed again as she yelled after the dis-
appearing figure, "Stop, damn you!"

But he kept on going and didn't turn back.

Niera reminded herself that she was on her own. The
FBI had already held a memorial service for Royce Taggart.

The next morning, a female agent brought from Niera's apartment some old clothing and a battered winter coat she hadn't worn in years, along with two new nightgowns and robes. She explained that Niera would be given expense money to buy new winter clothing as soon as she and Megan Overett were able to leave the hospital in Montana.

Her purse—the same fawn-colored leather shoulder bag she'd carried on the night of the explosion—had obviously been searched. The seams had been torn out and sloppily resewn before the FBI had returned it to her.

Two other agents met her plane in Los Angeles, where she was transferred to a flight for Billings.

Actually, by her count, *three* other agents were there. Once again, she caught a brief glimpse of the newly blond Royce just before her wheelchair was maneuvered in the opposite direction. By the time her frantic demands convinced the agent piloting her to turn her back around, Royce had dissolved into the crowd.

Chapter 1

"MAYBE IT WASN'T Royce you saw at the airport," Megan Overett said sympathetically.

"That's possible. I just caught a quick glimpse," Niera admitted to the woman who had become her close friend. "But I *am* a trained observer. And I had seen him twice before, on the hospital grounds."

She glanced out the window of the cabin they were sharing near Glacier National Park in the mountains of Montana, remembering the abundant tropical beauty of Hawaii. Now she saw only wide stretches of deep snow, studded with tops of tall evergreens. If only it were white sand dotted with swaying palm trees.

She sighed audibly before looking back to Megan. The one positive element in her life now was her friendship with the younger woman. The first time Niera had met her, Megan had looked about sixteen, although she was, in fact, twenty-three. Her freckles had stood out on pale skin below her short-cropped reddish hair, and her tall figure was painfully thin, for she had just been moved out of intensive care.

Megan and her husband had tried to foil the kidnapping of the teenage son of a wealthy businessman who owned a chain of pizza parlors. As they'd rounded a corner to enter one of those restaurants, they'd seen the screaming teenager being bundled into a van. Not knowing exactly what was going on, or that the two men were armed and that there was a third man unseen inside the van, Megan's husband had tried to help the boy. He had been shot on the spot, and the kidnappers had turned their guns on Megan to eliminate the witness. She had caught one bullet before she ducked around the corner to safety, and the van had raced off into the night. Megan's engineer husband of less than a year had died immediately.

There was a possibility that the kidnapping was connected to organized crime, which had been trying to move in on privately owned restaurant chains in the Midwest. That aspect, along with the viciousness of the killers, had persuaded the FBI to provide protection for Megan at least until the kidnappers were caught, and continued protection along with eventual relocation if organized crime did prove to be involved.

Niera hadn't realized how much she'd missed having close female confidants. Early in her career, she'd moved around too much to establish long-term relationships with either men or women. Most of the people she saw were colleagues, and nearly all of them were men. It was department practice to assign female agents with male partners.

Although she and Megan had been on cordial terms from the start, most of the efforts of genuine closeness had been initiated by Megan. Niera had spent many years concealing a part of herself and refusing to trust people. Now she found it hard to drop her guard with a comparative stranger all at once. Sometimes she wasn't sure that even she knew who the real Niera Pascotti was anymore.

It took almost three months for Niera to feel comfortable discussing her innermost feelings with Megan.

They had been moved to this remote area after their recovery. Here in the snowbound cabin, they jogged in place and rode a stationary bicycle to stay in shape.

The cabin had two bedrooms—one for her and Megan, and one for the two male agents assigned to "protect the witness."

During this entire period, Niera hadn't lost sight of the fact that she was as much the guarded as the guard. She hadn't been allowed to return to Honolulu, and she could learn only that all the leads had come to a dead end, and no arrests had been made.

She couldn't believe that all of her work, and Royce's, had led nowhere. She wanted desperately to get back to Honolulu and follow through on the investigation herself now that she was well again. She even considered resigning so that she could follow through as a private citizen, but then she'd lack the considerable resources of the FBI. So she was biding her time a little longer.

Besides, Megan needed her. It was wrenching enough to have to adjust to the loss of a husband she'd loved very much without being stuck away in a lonely cabin with no other woman to talk to.

And Niera had only recently acknowledged how badly she herself had needed a friend like Megan.

She wouldn't desert Megan as long as she had a choice.

But who was helping whom? Niera wondered, as Megan gently persisted with their discussion. Niera had finally trusted Megan enough to tell her about having seen Royce those three times. She wouldn't have told anyone else for fear of being considered crazy, or at least not fully recovered from the minor concussion she'd suffered in the explosion.

Sitting on the edge of her bed, Megan leaned sympathetically toward Niera. "I know you truly believe you saw Royce." She added hesitantly, "I know—because you wouldn't believe how many times I've seen Daniel."

At Niera's puzzled expression, Megan continued, "I saw him in the hospital—in the corridors, in the lobby, outside on the grounds. Later on, I saw him again, at the general store where we stopped on our way to this cabin." She took a deep breath. "I would catch sight of something familiar. Some sort of resemblance in height or build or hair color or facial structure. The way he walked, the sound of his voice, the way he laughed. For an instant, my heart stops and joy races through my veins, because I know that Daniel is really alive, right there."

A tear slipped out of one of Megan's dark blue eyes and rolled down over the freckles on her cheek. Niera felt terrible that discussing her own problems had brought Megan such grief. All she could say was, "I'm sorry."

"You must understand—we must both understand—that these reactions are normal. I know all about denial, about wishing and hoping and dreaming. And I saw Daniel fall to the ground. I saw—" She hesitated, swallowing hard. "Still, a part of me won't accept the fact that I'll never see him again."

"But you loved Daniel very much. I wasn't in love with Royce."

"But you said you were attracted to him and that you cared for him."

"I did *like* him. If we'd had more time, or if I hadn't held back so much of myself, maybe I *could* have loved him. But the fact is, I didn't."

"But you do feel guilty over his death, if for no other

reason than because you were his partner, and partners are supposed to protect each other." Megan's statement was an observation rather than a question.

"Of course. I still wonder if I could have done something different . . ."

"Just as I wonder if I could have stopped Daniel, or been alert enough to see the gun or the third man in time to warn him. Something, anything."

"You couldn't have."

"Neither could you," Megan pointed out softly. "But if you convince yourself that Royce is alive, you don't have to deal with so much guilt—for not having been able to prevent Royce's death and for not loving him even as much as he loved you." She paused, then added, "And maybe you're not confronting the similarities between this and your memories of Sam."

"I'm not emotionally available," Niera murmured. It was a catchphrase they'd picked up from watching a television talk show on love relationships. In their later conversations, Niera had come to realize that it applied to her personal life.

She had always felt that Sam Draper was her great true love, even though they'd had no permanent commitment. She had experienced the full whirlpool of emotions that a young college sophomore could feel over an older, more mature student. Sam had been going to law school part time and supporting himself by working as a police officer. He was called one night to the site of a bomb threat. The threat and the bomb were real, and in a millisecond Sam Draper ceased to exist.

Her discussions with Megan had helped Niera to recognize that during the years she'd held on to her love for Sam Draper, she hadn't been emotionally available to anyone else. And she now understood that perhaps she had been attracted to Sam in the first place because, like her, he wasn't fully emotionally available. He'd wanted to complete law school and become established in his career before he married. So he'd been a safe choice for Niera, who really didn't want to get married either.

The couple of men she'd harbored special feelings for later on actually hadn't been available either. She'd thought she cared for a protected witness several years earlier, but Lincoln Stanford had been nurturing his love for a woman he hadn't told even the FBI about in order to ensure her safety.

A subsequent romance never really got off the ground because of conflicting career demands.

And she hadn't loved Royce Taggart.

But she wanted to be in love. Like Linc and Kelly. Like John and Lisa. Like Megan and Daniel.

Maybe now, due to her enforced vacation of sorts and the valuable insights she'd gained from her serious conversations with Megan, maybe now she was ready to fall in love.

"They struck a deal. And it's all over," Megan repeated in shocked disbelief when a courier arrived with the news a couple of mornings later. "All of this, all this time, and suddenly I'm free to do whatever I want, go wherever I want." The words were forced out of Megan's firmly set lips. "And Daniel died for nothing. For nothing."

Niera moved quickly to comfort her. "Daniel believed he was helping that boy."

The FBI courier had come to the cabin with the proverbial good news and bad news. The spoiled teenager, miffed that his father wouldn't buy him a second sports car after he'd wrecked the first, had faked his own kidnapping as a way of getting extra money while striking back at his father. His cohorts had panicked and fired when Daniel and Megan saw them. Finally, the FBI had caught up with them, and they'd confessed all in a plea bargain for reduced charges. Organized crime had not been involved.

Megan was still moving like a zombie when they all left the cabin behind and drove to Great Falls to spend the night at a hotel before going their separate ways.

Niera telephoned Hal, hoping he was ready to let her return to Honolulu. She wanted to take Megan with her. They could share her apartment for a while.

Then she realized she'd be placing Megan in new danger, both from the criminals she was currently investigating and from every other felon she'd ever run to ground. As an FBI agent, she never knew when she might become the hunted as well as the hunter. The counterfeit merchandise ring might already have murdered one agent. She wouldn't place Megan at risk.

From the other end of the line, Hal was saying, "This came up so suddenly. You've got several weeks of accrued vacation time. I'm scheduling you for some of it now."

Niera recognized the stall. In other words, they had no additional evidence to implicate her, but they hadn't found evidence to clear her, either.

Well, millions of people took their vacations in Hawaii, she reminded herself. There was no reason why Niera Pascotti couldn't be one of them.

But then Hal said, "By the way, I want you to relax and enjoy yourself." He paused before adding the unmistakable clarification, "Don't spend your vacation hanging around your usual stomping grounds here in Hawaii. Let us know where you'll be."

He was indirectly ordering her not to return to Hawaii yet. She would have to decide whether to ignore that and pursue the case on her own or whether to obey Hal's order and keep her job for the present, hoping that some other agent would eventually catch the real criminals and clear her. Niera decided to sleep on the decision.

* * *

By the next morning, Megan had recovered some-what from her series of shocks on the prior day. "Are you going back to Honolulu?" she asked.

Niera related her conversation with Hal and its impli-cations, neglecting to mention that she hadn't made a final decision.

Megan walked over to the desk in the hotel room as she voiced her thoughts. "If you wouldn't mind my tag-ging along, it would be really good for me to come with you. Separate vacations, but sort of together."

"What does that mean?"

"I need to ease back into society, so I shouldn't de-pend too much on you. Maybe we could take a cruise, where a lot of other people are around and there are group tours at the stops. Then I'd be able to get reac-customed to social situations. But you'd be on the same ship if we needed each other—I mean, if I needed you."

Once again, Niera wondered who was helping whom. The same type of vacation that would be good for Megan would be good for her also, she realized. Her leads in the merchandise-counterfeiting case had been cooling for three months. A couple of additional weeks wouldn't make any difference, especially since Hal had claimed that all the leads in her reports had been inves-tigated already.

"Eventually, I'll have to decide what an unskilled person with a liberal arts degree can do for a living," Megan said. "But I'm financially well off for now, with my trust fund and Daniel's insurance. So I can afford to go anywhere you choose. And it's about time I had a real vacation."

With growing enthusiasm, they discussed their vaca-tion ideas.

"The two of us can travel together," Niera said. "We don't have to stay apart."

"I meant it when I said that semi-private would be

best for me. I feel sort of like a trapeze artist who's ready to perform again, but not without a net. You'll be my net. I'll know you're there, but I'll make a real effort to mingle with other people." Megan glanced wistfully out the window. "I used to be very shy. Daniel was helping me get over that."

"You sure this is what you want?"

"Positive. I'm not ready to love again. Not yet. But I need to be around groups of people now. We can have separate staterooms, and meet at least once a day."

"Okay." Niera wasn't certain how much her agreement was for Megan's sake and how much for her own.

"And starting now," Megan declared, glancing at her watch, "we both live only in the present moment."

"Agreed."

Two hours later, they were at a travel agency looking through stacks of cruise brochures. The Caribbean. The Greek Isles. The Orient. Across the Atlantic. The South Pacific.

"I don't really care. I talked you into this, so you pick the destination," Megan said. "Just like Dorothy, I'd never been out of Kansas until Daniel and I honeymooned in London. Any place is Oz as far as I'm concerned."

Then let's pick one where we won't run into any wicked witches, Niera thought. She knew where the high crime rates were, where drug traffic flourished, where terrorists operated most freely.

But she also knew of one isolated part of the world that was fairly free of all that, where she could truly count on a safe and peaceful vacation. And most of the islands where that cruise ship stopped were tiny and sparsely populated. That meant she would be able to track down a certain blond man if she chanced to catch a glimpse of him.

Niera firmly shook that thought out of her head. Along with Megan, she'd vowed to live in the present.

There would be no familiar-looking man for the next couple of weeks.

"I propose French Polynesia—Tahiti and its neighbor islands." She waved a brochure under Megan's pert nose. "Bora Bora, Huahiné, Raiatéa, and Mooréa—and they all look as exotically lovely as they sound."

The travel agent interjected, "People tend to refer to the entire area as Tahiti, even though that's technically the name of only one of the islands in French Polynesia." She launched into a fact-filled sales pitch. "The islands are located in the middle of the Pacific, halfway between California and Australia, and twenty-five hundred miles south of Hawaii." She smiled at them. "That's about as far from everything as it's possible to get. And the islands are almost totally crime-free, except in Papeete, the capital of Tahiti."

"Sounds like our kind of place," Megan said, as her eyes met Niera's in mutual understanding.

They learned that a cruise was presently in progress, and they would have to wait almost a week before the next one started. They decided, instead of waiting, to fly to French Polynesia.

"I don't know if we want to spend extra time on the island of Tahiti, though," Niera said. "Papeete is known as a rough little seaport. I'm sure parts of it are dangerous at times."

"Bora Bora is noted for its diving and its beauty," the travel agent said. "You could connect with the ship there if you'd prefer, but you'd miss a whole day of sailing while the ship is traveling from Tahiti to Bora Bora."

Niera and Megan immediately agreed on Bora Bora and made the arrangements.

Adjusting her snorkeling mask, Niera spun around

slowly in sheer delight, her arms spread wide as if to encompass the underwater panoramas around her.

She was smack dab in the middle of the sea!

Or so it seemed, anyway, as she hovered over the apex of a hill among the underwater rises and valleys. A short distance above her head, she could see white foam signaling the arrival of waves from thousands of miles across the ocean. Nestled in the protective embrace of the barrier reef, she studied the gentle lagoon that encircled the island, sparkling with a spectrum of blues. Beyond the bay, the mountainous center of Bora Bora rose like a broad green exclamation point on the horizon.

Beyond the cove, she could glimpse the cruise ship. From the balcony of her hotel room that morning, she had seen the gleaming white vessel emerge from the mists of dawn. Now it floated off-shore like a lazy leviathan. Since early morning, the ship's tenders had been ferrying passengers to the island.

This sudden increase in the island's population was reflected by the number of small boats dotting the surrounding sea, although it was still far from jammed.

Drifting nearby was an outrigger canoe, which Niera had rented, complete with Tahitian boatman, from her hotel. She and Megan hadn't ventured far from the hotel during their three days here, but they had occasionally gone swimming and snorkeling during those rare periods when it wasn't raining.

Since Bora Bora offered some of the world's best underwater sight-seeing, Niera had decided to snorkel one last time before sending her luggage out to the ship and spending the balance of the day wandering around the island. Megan already had joined a group tour of passengers from the ship.

Niera could have taken the boat out alone, but solitary snorkeling could be hazardous, and her motto was "No unnecessary risks." The key word was *unnecessary*. Although her job was hazardous, she considered those well-calculated risks essential.

She didn't want to think about her job today. She didn't want to think about anything, really, except the present moment.

Looking down through the transparent water, she laughed at the huge black rubber swim fins on her feet. They looked like ridiculous clown shoes. But besides facilitating her movement through the water, they protected the soles of her feet against toxic sea urchins, sharp rocks, and the like.

Flashes of jonquil nearby caught her attention. After quickly replacing her glass snorkeling mask, with its tall rubber tube, and tugging on her raspberry-colored bikini, she paddled in that direction.

But for its liquid warmth and buoyancy, the water might have been nonexistent. To deem it as clear as crystal would be incorrect, Niera mused. She could not have seen distinctly through ninety feet of glass, and yet she could view the sandy bottom of this lagoon at even greater distances.

As she undulated through this exotic world, she'd pretended she was part of it. A carefree water nymph.

But she wasn't part of it. Not really. She was only a spectator peering at this uncomplicated elegance. An outsider looking in, her nose pressed against the glass almost literally.

She wanted to be a part of something. She wanted to belong somewhere.

Perhaps she could find the real Niera Pascotti here, in this primeval environment. For those several days, the relentless FBI investigator did not exist. Instead, there was merely Niera Pascotti, human being.

Was she postponing her life? Or finally starting it?

For the moment, she found joy in trailing after a school of butterfly fish with bright yellow tails on their zebra-striped bodies.

The vivid fish headed around a submerged wall of coral. As Niera rounded the outcropping of coral after them, something enormous struck her from below.

The impact, coupled with the flow of the current, propelled her toward the dangerous serrated coral. And a shadowy figure nearby made her fear she'd been attacked by a shark.

But it was a man who reached out for her, pulling her back, away from the jagged coral. His quick action saved her from nasty gashes and infection.

She registered the overall impression of a lightly tanned male chest and arms, emerald-green swim trunks, and scuba tanks. He must have been closing in on the butterfly fish from the opposite direction.

She wanted to thank him for pulling her back from the coral, but the air piece in her mouth had the effect of a gag. She lifted one hand, pointing upward, then kicked her way to the surface, beckoning him to follow.

As they broke the surface close to each other, the water washed over and ran off their face masks like a torrent of rain cascading down a windowpane.

Like the rain washing over the hospital windowpane that day in Honolulu.

Royce! Dark blond hair, wet, was flattened against his head. Aquamarine eyes widened in amazement as he seemed to recognize her, also.

Yanking his regulator out of his mouth, he asked in a rush, "Are you all right?"

She managed to nod affirmatively.

Before she had a chance to speak, he replaced his regulator and dived beneath the surface.

He isn't getting away from me this time, Niera vowed. She was a good swimmer, and her leg was now fully healed.

Putting all her might into her strokes, she pursued Royce. He immediately headed for the deepest area, accessible with his scuba equipment. But she was able to keep him in view through her glass face mask.

He twisted his way through the labyrinths of coral, swimming so close to the jagged projections that she feared he would be ripped apart.

Still she followed, staying close to the surface above him. Her arms ached with the effort, and she willed her legs not to cramp.

She had to keep him in sight. She couldn't let him get away. Niera forced herself to keep swimming despite her aching muscles, scarcely aware of the varieties of brilliantly hued fish crossing her path.

Half a dozen stingrays glided in graceful formation just above the buff-colored sandy bottom. If they'd been nearer the surface, Niera might have been tempted to hitch a ride on a stingray, as she'd been told was possible. Instead, they served to remind her that, despite the beauty, myriad dangers lurked in these deceptively placid depths.

Fatigue was sapping her strength. Still, she forced herself forward. His lead had increased only slightly.

They reached the barrier reef enclosing the lagoon. He seemed trapped between the fortress of coral ahead, and Niera above and behind.

She could almost sense his panic as he propelled himself along the wall of coral like a cornered animal.

Then he found the gap he sought. He slipped through it into the ocean beyond.

Damn! And double damn. And ancient Polynesian curses, if she'd known any.

Niera knew it would be impossible to keep up with him in the open sea with only snorkeling gear. And exhaustion was weighing on her like stones. She gave a long sigh of frustration and disgust.

Approaching the reef carefully, she stood atop the

jagged coral with the armor of thick black rubber insulating her feet. Jerking off her snorkeling mask, she scanned the ocean for a sign of the man. She saw only rippling waves spangled with sunlight.

She turned to face the other direction. Her outrigger was in sight. The boatman started toward her as soon as she beckoned.

She considered flinging herself into the canoe and yelling, "Follow that scuba diver." But she already knew, with a sagging sense of defeat, that chasing him would be futile.

She pulled herself into the metal outrigger. Yanking off her swim fins, she threw them down with an angry slap.

The boatman regarded her with puzzlement. She understood the gist of his question in French as to whether or not she'd enjoyed her morning.

In a voice crisp with disappointment, she mumbled to the uncomprehending boatman, "You should have seen the one that got away."

In fact, she supposed the boatman hadn't been close enough to see him at all.

But he was no misplaced merman. No figment of her imagination.

Or was he?

True, she had encountered a blond scuba diver who sounded like an American. But was she exaggerating other similarities between him and Royce, between him and assorted other blond strangers?

The breeze murmured taunts in her ears like phantoms on the wind, as the outrigger skimmed toward shore.

Resting her chin on her folded arms along the gunwales of the outrigger, she stared into the water, trying to collect her thoughts and plan her next moves.

In the undersea tableau, black slits that looked like snakes denoted the partly opened mouths of clams locked within the coral's fatal grip. They were trapped there for all time, but they could stay alive indefinitely, eating through those slits.

At the moment, Niera felt equally imprisoned. No matter where on earth or sea she tried to escape, she couldn't shake free of her past, her ghosts, the intrigues grasping at her.

Those black slits, those perpetually half-open mouths, seemed like unending silent screams.

Like her own unending silent scream.

Chapter 2

NIERA PARKED HER rented bicycle alongside several others, then straightened her peach-colored shorts and flowered shirt. The ground coral covering Bora Bora's slender main road crunched beneath her sandals as she crossed to the wooden archway proclaiming BLOODY MARY'S. She might as well experience the closest thing Bora Bora had to a tourist trap.

She'd decided against trying to locate the blond man in her remaining hours on Bora Bora. If he was a figment of her imagination, perhaps she'd never see him again. If he was real, perhaps he'd make an appearance on the ship. Either way, she intended to get on with her vacation. In fact, she mused uncomfortably, she was now determined to pursue pleasure with the same relentlessness and single-mindedness that she normally devoted to a case.

She'd decided not to mention this morning's encounter to Megan unless she saw the man again. But if she did glimpse a blond version of Royce on the cruise, she'd tear the ship apart from fore to aft, starboard to port, and whatever other directions ships came in.

As she entered the restaurant, Niera blinked at the dimness and the dense haze of smoke. Her first reaction was that she had entered the prototype for seedy South Seas bars. Although it was barely lunchtime, the interior was dark. The only illumination was a streak of daylight sneaking feebly through three feet of open space between the sandy floor and the low-hanging palm-thatch roof.

Niera was tempted to grab the hostess so as not to get lost on her way to the table. Coughing as the smoke grew so heavy it seemed almost solid, she realized they were passing a large, unvented charcoal grill.

She was reminded of the cap of a mushroom as she perched on a stool made of an upright, varnished section of palm trunk. Shellacked palm logs, split lengthwise, provided the tabletop.

Her burning eyes struggled to adjust to the darkness. She closed them for a few seconds, fighting back the protective tears. When she opened her eyes again, the room gradually came into focus.

The next time she blinked, it was in disbelief at the sight coming toward her.

Blond hair, medium height—

Her breath caught in her throat, and her heart hammered a wild rhythm. Despite the darkness, she was certain he was the same man she'd pursued across the lagoon that morning.

She started to rise to go after him, but it wasn't necessary.

He stopped at her table!

"Excuse me," he said, "it's so dark in here that I can't tell for sure—but aren't you the lady who was snorkeling by the barrier reef this morning?"

Astonished at his boldness in confronting her directly, she leashed her excitement at a chance to finally speak with him. "Yes, I am," she managed to answer calmly. She added with studied nonchalance, "I thought you looked familiar."

"Between the dim lighting here and the diving masks earlier, we're hard to recognize." His reply came easily. "Mind if I join you?"

"Please do." She'd been waiting for him to join her for three months.

As he balanced his larger frame on the stool across from her, she asked casually, "Why have you been running away from me?"

He hesitated before replying, "Running away?"

She had assumed that was how he'd play it. Much as she'd love to leap across the table, grab him by the throat, and demand that he admit he was Royce Taggart, such actions would be pointless. He'd hardly confess simply because she asked him directly, when it was obvious that he planned to carry out a pretense.

It was insulting that Royce underestimated her ability to recognize him despite cosmetic changes in his appearance. Was he still working with the FBI, hoping to lure her into revealing her supposed involvement with the criminals? Or was he acting on his own, following her because he believed she'd been criminally involved in the counterfeiting—maybe even responsible for the explosion?

Studying him through the murky haze, she thought his features might not be quite the same as she remembered, but she couldn't see well enough to be sure.

There were other possibilities. She had informed the Honolulu and Los Angeles offices of the FBI that she'd be taking this cruise. Maybe some of the other agents had been aware of the developing relationship between herself and Royce; perhaps they'd chosen an agent who strongly resembled Royce in the hope that she'd reveal incriminating information to him. Technically, the FBI wasn't allowed to operate outside the United States, but another agent could be "on vacation," too. She could be the target of a modern FBI version of *Gaslight:* Make the lady think she's crazy.

No, I'm not crazy. And I'm not imagining the resemblance. Niera had to continue believing in herself.

But for now she'd play this cat-and-mouse game his way, to a degree. Scarcely missing a beat, she picked up the thread of casual conversation. "You rushed away this morning when I wanted to thank you for pulling me back from the coral."

"No thanks are necessary," he said easily. "It was my fault for crashing into you. I guess we were both intent on watching the same fish, and peripheral vision isn't too good with those diving masks."

"Why didn't you stop when I was trying to catch up with you?"

"Were you? Those masks aren't equipped with rear-view mirrors, either." He maintained a blank expression. "Sorry."

The waitress interrupted. Niera ordered a Mai Tai, the house special. He said he had to try a Bloody Mary at Bloody Mary's. There was little choice for an entrée: Grouper was the catch of the day.

As they chatted about the lovely weather, Niera concentrated on his voice. It was deep, but huskier than she recalled. Still, the smoke in this restaurant would make any throat husky. She herself expected to leave sounding like Lauren Bacall.

"Wouldn't you know it?" he remarked when the waitress brought their drinks. "A tribute to the far-reaching influence of American show business. Blood Marys at Blood Mary's are served in red, white, and blue paper cups. Our toast is predetermined." He picked up his drink, which was garnished with a slice of cucumber. "To Rodgers and Hammerstein."

Hoisting her Mai Tai, with its pineapple chunk perched on the rim, she noticed that he held his cup in his right hand. Royce was right-handed, but so was most of the world.

Their fingers brushed.

After their inaugural sips, she said, "We must have one more toast. Why does everyone always forget the original writers? To James Michener."

This time, the contact of their fingers was intentional. Excitement crackled through her as they remained touching longer than necessary.

At last, he lifted his cup to his lips, murmuring, "To Jimmy, then, for using Bora Bora as the model for Bali Ha'i in *Tales of the South Pacific*."

A tune from that musical, "Some Enchanted Evening," began wafting through her mind.

In some ways, this afternoon did seem enchanted. If only she could give in to it, if only this man would stop pretending to be a stranger.

He was continuing their earlier discussion. "They might not have known what to name tourist accommodations here if it hadn't been for Michener and Rodgers and Hammerstein. *South Pacific* spawned the chain of the Bali Ha'i Hotels, Bloody Mary's—"

"Speaking of names," she interrupted, "do you have one, or are you waiting for the musical?"

"Cort Tucker," he answered promptly, just the way a good undercover agent would. "How about you?"

"Mitzi Gaynor," she said dryly.

He laughed, affording her a glimpse of his matching dimples. "Well, Mitzi, I adore women with clean hair." Then his voice caught before he added, "Got that man washed out of it yet?"

She shrugged. "I could always wear a wig. Camouflage is all the rage nowadays."

"It would be too bad," he said softly, "to cover up your hair. It looks like spun sunshine."

She refused to succumb to flattery. "It isn't brightening this room much." And she certainly longed for more illumination.

She shifted her strategy. "Michener described Bora Bora as the most spectacular island in the world. It's attractive, but from what I've seen so far, I'd say most of the Hawaiian islands are much more beautiful." She watched intently for his reaction. "What do you think?"

The pause was almost tangible before he replied, "I've never been to Hawaii."

"It's fabulous. You ought to try it sometime." She noted that he hadn't asked the usual questions as to how she was familiar with Hawaii.

"Maybe I'll try Hawaii on my vacation," he said.

"You mean on your *next* vacation? Surely you're not working now." What unusual cover story had he concocted to explain his presence in laid-back French Polynesia?

"Actually, I am here on business."

She couldn't help drawing a deep, expectant breath.

He continued, "I'm exploring how Tahitian *pareos* might be adapted for American women. *Pareos* are those long, colorful strips of cloth that can be wrapped several ways as dresses."

Disappointment washed over her. What had she expected? she chided herself. Instant true confessions? At least his story fit the locale. And provided an excuse for him to watch lots of women besides her. Why did that last thought disturb her?

She said distractedly, *"Pareos* are rather revealing garments from what I've seen so far. And when Dorothy Lamour wore them in old movies, they were called sarongs."

"Well, I plan to decide whether two sarongs can make a right."

Smiling, she offered in mock sympathy, "It must be grueling to do the product and the market research."

"Absolutely terrible." He nodded in agreement. He fumbled with his napkin before asking, "What about you, Mitzi? What do you do when you're not singing and dancing?"

"Or washing my hair?" she said jokingly. "Actually, I'm between jobs now." That was possibly the first accurate personal fact to surface in this entire conversation, she mused.

"What kind of jobs are you between?"

"You could call it research, mostly." *Research* was as good a euphemism as any for *investigation*. "Do you suppose your employer might have a spot for another researcher?"

He was hit by a spasm of coughing. "Sorry," he hacked out when he was through. "I don't know if that was the drink or the smoke."

Niera refrained from pointing out a third probability. She prodded again, "Who *is* your employer?"

"If you're hoping to do me out of a job, I'm afraid it won't work. I'm my own employer."

"How interesting," she murmured. The comment had the desired effect of making him explain further.

"I have other personnel, but I don't have any openings now."

"Too bad. And I suppose you're intent on doing all the *pareo* research personally."

"Maybe I could use a m-model," he stammered.

A strange warmth suffused her at realizing that he seemed unaccustomed to handing out such lines. She said simply, "That's nice," adding, "and maybe I could check with you sometime in the future about other positions. Do you have a business card?"

"Sorry. I left them on the ship."

"So you're on the cruise." She paused before persisting, "What and where is your business?"

He answered promptly, "I own Dressed for Excess, with headquarters in Denver. I'm a national distributor and manufacturer of women's specialty clothing—particularly lounge and evening wear."

Now it was Niera's turn to nearly choke on her drink. She would have expected a cover story further removed from the actual case.

"You okay?" Cort asked.

Her head bobbed up and down in reply.

"Now that you know the story of my life, Mitzi, do you perchance have another name?"

"Niera Pascotti, from Hawaii." She extended her hand.

The handshake far surpassed how-do-you-do. Cort did very well, his firm grasp launching zinging sensations throughout her body. Their hands remained cradled together while seconds ticked past.

The lingering touch was broken by the waitress serving their dinner.

The shock of that brief contact had been as disconcerting to Niera's body as another shock was to her mind: When she withdrew her hand in what she hoped would appear to be a slow caress, she felt no calluses. Cort's fingers were corporate-executive smooth.

But three months had passed, she reminded herself. Royce's calluses could have vanished by now.

Casting about for chit-chat to conceal her discomfiture, she pointed out the forest-green leaves resting between their grilled fish and the metal plates. "Traditionally, Tahitian meals are served on leaves. These are *porou* leaves. Every part of the *porou* tree, including the yellow flowers, provides something useful."

He touched the leaves. "Sort of the tropical equivalent of a paper plate, to match the paper cups I suppose," he kidded.

"I say, avoid washing dishes any way you can. I guess housewives on Bora Bora even have a good excuse, because there's such a shortage of fresh water here."

"Having my own talking guidebook is a treat." His comment had a veneer of sincerity. "How do you know so much?"

"Hope I don't bore you." She felt a flicker of annoyance with herself when she realized that was absolutely true. She didn't want this man to consider her dull.

"No way are you boring me," he assured her.

She didn't explain that she'd had ample opportunity for reading in her hotel room during the frequent rainstorms, telling him only, "I guess I've learned a few things in my four days here."

"So that's where you've been." As soon as he spoke, he bit his lip, as if the remark had popped out and he wished he could retrieve it.

She pounced on it. "What do you mean?"

"I, uh, just meant—"

Niera thought his verbal fumbling was odd. Royce was an experienced agent, practiced in telling lies and guarding secrets.

"I meant," he recovered, "that's why I didn't see you on the ship yesterday."

"You wouldn't necessarily have seen me among hundreds of people."

"But I would have remembered you if I had."

Niera tried to convince herself that the silkiness of his comment was disgusting.

"Maybe," he ventured, "I should jump ship and stay on Bora Bora."

"I'd be sorry to see that happen," she said honestly. "I'll be joining the cruise." She might as well make it easy for him to follow her, now that he'd established contact. That could only simplify her own "research."

Niera scarcely tasted the fish and rice as they chatted about a variety of trivia while they ate. For dessert, they savored a specialty ice cream concocted of fresh coconut and coconut milk.

She declined his offer to pay for her lunch, and noticed that he paid for his own with cash. A credit card would have been more likely if he were really on a tax-deductible business trip.

Her heart thumped in her eagerness to walk into the bright sunlight with him.

Rising and turning, he noticed the small illumined sign on the overhanging thatch above the restaurant. *"Sortie de Secours,"* he read aloud. "It's been a long time since my last buying trip to Paris, but doesn't that mean Emergency Exit?"

"Right," she confirmed with a grin.

"But the whole restaurant is open-sided," he said, puzzled. "You could leave anywhere."

"I heard an explanation my first day on Bora Bora," she told him. "Regulations state that a restaurant must have emergency exits posted. The French bureaucrats wouldn't give Bloody Mary's a permit to open until the specified number of emergency exit signs were hanging in place."

He laughed, and Niera thought again what a wonderful, deep, husky laugh he had. "Do you get a mental picture," he said, "of dozens of French bureaucrats piled on top of one another, all trying to leave properly from beneath that sign in an emergency?"

She accompanied him out of the restaurant, and they strolled into the stark glare of sunlight. Temporarily blinded by that brilliant orb suspended in an azure sky, Niera squinted. Cort was squinting, too, shielding his eyes with his left hand.

Finally their gazes merged, together growing accustomed to the brightness. And to each other.

She had only quickly registered his eye color that morning through the glass diving masks and had thought the greenish tinge might be merely the sea's reflection.

Now, looking at him in full daylight, she saw that the color had not been an illusion.

Cort's eyes were a languorous aquamarine. Royce's eyes had been pale blue.

She stared more closely, hoping to discern the outline of contact lenses. But if he was wearing them, they weren't easy to spot. Of course, eye color could be changed by injecting dye into the irises, although Niera doubted her case was important enough to warrant such a drastic measure.

Sunbeams frolicked among the intermingling shades of blond in his hair, from fine cornsilk to winter wheat. The overall effect, she noticed, was a darker blond than her own. Niera realized she was searching for roots of a different hue—dark brown roots that might have emerged since the last bleaching. She saw none.

His jaw still had the same strong, attractive curve, although tension drew the chin more taut than she remembered its being. His nose seemed a bit shorter than she recalled, and it was also a tad crooked. But perhaps it just looked different now that his mustache was gone. Or maybe his nose was broken in the explosion. Maybe he, too, was knocked down by the shock waves or hit by debris.

He was barely tanned; but Royce's tan could have faded by now. Cort did seem leaner than Royce, though just as fit. His arms looked strong, but they were not as blatantly muscled. His garb was typically touristy—a loose-fitting red print shirt and red shorts. She didn't mind admiring his legs.

As she tried to study him objectively, a tingle rose within her and spiraled throughout her being until every cell seemed to vibrate with awareness of him. In any guise, he was a very attractive man.

Perhaps misinterpreting her prolonged gaze, he reached over and trailed his finger along her cheek. "At last," he murmured, "we meet close up." An instant later, he added, gesturing toward the restaurant, "Without the darkness and the haze, I mean."

Oh, there was still a haze all right, Niera thought. A haze of memories, a haze of uncertainties, swirling between them like a dense fog.

She noted her rapid heartbeat, her racing pulse. Why was she fantasizing being drawn into those arms, being kissed, again hearing the last words she'd heard that night? She knew this man was lying to her, playing games—even if he was under orders from the FBI.

Suddenly, Niera realized she desperately wanted to believe that Cort Tucker was really the accidental tourist his clothing and demeanor would indicate. She wanted to pretend, for a little while, that an appealing stranger might be interested in a woman he'd happened to run into, literally, off the coast of Bora Bora. But the similarities to Royce were too great.

Finally, he broke their gaze to stare out over the lagoon. "I rented a bicycle," he said. "The cars were all taken."

"So I discovered. I'm an itinerant pedaler myself."

"Would you like to join me for a ride? I was going to cycle all the way around the island, but that's a total of twenty-one miles. If you're not up to that, we could go a shorter distance."

How would he know she might not be capable of a long bike ride, unless he was aware of her recent injuries? Or did he chauvinistically doubt the stamina of all women?

"Around the island is fine." She'd been riding a stationery bicycle often as part of her physical therapy. At least they could continue going around in circles by the scenic route.

With the time difference, it was now late Friday afternoon in the United States. Niera wanted to make a telephone call to Denver, although she already knew what she would hear.

She excused herself on the pretext of returning inside to the ladies' room. But Cort followed her into the restaurant, so she had no chance to use the telephone without his knowing, and Bora Bora didn't exactly have a pay phone on every corner. In fact, it hardly had corners.

But at least he wouldn't get away from her again.

Chapter 3

"I CAME IN search of roots. Instead, I've found ruts," Niera remarked, as they jounced and bounced along on their bicycles.

"Thinking in terms of ancient gods, I've decided this must have been the washboard for the Polynesian equivalent of the Jolly Green Giant." He echoed her opinion of Bora Bora's only 'highway.' "What did you mean about roots?"

"The original Hawaiians migrated there from this group of islands."

Other than such occasional comments, they talked very little. But their silence was one of easy companionship. Niera felt that this level of comfortable companionship would be unusual for new acquaintances.

Topped with ground coral and shells, the narrow pearl-gray road unfolded before them like a length of grosgrain ribbon twining around a package of vivid greens and bright flowers. On one side of the road was the hilly center of Bora Bora. On the other side lay the vast lagoon with blues upon blues in ever-changing hues.

As they rode, the bicycle wheels hummed a slow melody, like stringed instruments over gentle percussion. They passed a series of tranquil coves and coconut groves at the base of the jungle-blanketed volcanic mountains that jutted straight toward the sky. Around each curve in the road, a new vista awaited them.

That wouldn't be a bad philosophy for life, Niera mused. Just revel in the present and always assume that something equally wonderful awaits around the next bend for the future.

"Oh, look," Niera and Cort exclaimed almost in unison, as they rounded another curve.

"This must be Matira Beach," he said.

"I think you're right." Niera followed him toward an outdoor market. Ahead of them hung the eye-catching displays of Tahitian vendors whose children scrambled and played nearby. Hundreds of *pareos*—long rectangles of brightly colored cloth—hung on lines strung between the palm trees, looking like remnants of rainbow and swatches of sunset. All the vivid colors of land and sea had been captured in these fabrics.

"Mind if I mix a little business with pleasure?" Cort asked her.

"That's why you're here, isn't it?" Her reply sounded sharper than she'd intended. She tempered it by adding, "Besides, I'd like to browse, too."

"Far be it from me to discourage a lady from shopping for clothes."

They pedaled into a cleared area that served as a parking lot of sorts. As they got off their bikes, a cramp stabbed into Niera's left leg. She couldn't help crying out a long "ooooh!" as her face contorted with the unexpected pain. Only by leaning all her weight on the handlebars of the bicycle could she keep from slumping to the ground.

Cort was at her side in a second. "What is it? What's wrong?"

Her teeth were clenched too tightly together for her to speak. Her leg felt as if it were clamped in a vise.

"Are you all right?" Anxiety pulsed through his words. "Is it your leg?"

She nodded in answer to his last question. She decided it didn't necessarily require foreknowledge, since she had obviously shifted all her weight off that currently useless leg.

"Lean on me." He encircled her waist with one arm while steadying her bicycle with the other.

She wasn't accustomed to leaning on anybody at any time for any reason. But she was in too much pain to tell him that. It seemed so much easier to slip one arm around his strong shoulders and relax against him.

He scooped her up in his arms, letting her bicycle fall on the grass.

For a moment, she allowed Cort to cradle her against him, her soft breast pressed against the firmness of his chest, her cheek nestled in the arc of his neck.

The muscle spasms in her calf began to lessen, ebbing like an outgoing tide.

"It's better," she told him, suddenly more comfortable with the power of his arms than with the lack of power in her leg.

He ignored her comment, continuing toward his goal, a fallen palm tree whose thick trunk spanned the slender strip of champagne-colored sand and extended out over the aqua water.

He set her down on the palm trunk, and perhaps they were a little slower than necessary in letting go of each other.

"Thank you," she stammered as his ear passed near her lips. Noting that he smelled like coconuts, she wondered if she had consumed too much of that particular item in her days here. Maybe there was something to the phrase "going coconuts." Then she realized that he must have used a coconut-oil-based suntan lotion.

He knelt in front of her on one knee, and the classic proposal scene flashed unbidden into her mind. But, she reminded herself, she was no Cinderella, and Prince Charming could be working under an alias.

"That isn't necessary," she said in a rush when he lifted her leg and balanced her ankle on his thigh. The contact of flesh on flesh, her smooth skin against his hair-roughened thigh, sent bolts of electricity through her that could have zapped out any residual pain.

"Let me know if I'm making it worse," he said, beginning a tender massage with his thumbs on the still-tight muscles in her calf, his fingertips resting lightly on her leg.

She drew a deep breath at the impact of his touch, and her heart skipped into a crazy rhythm.

Instantly aware of her reaction, he misinterpreted it. "Did I hurt you?"

She shook her head. Disconcerted at her vulnerability to him, she vowed to be on guard at all times, never letting him get close enough to hurt her.

No pain, no gain, she thought, remembering the admonishment of her physical therapist in Great Falls. If she remained "not emotionally available," she might avoid being hurt, but she would also forfeit the heights of ecstasy.

Her brief pain of a few minutes ago certainly had resulted in immediate gain. Cort's thumbs, moving in deep caresses, easing out all the tension and all the kinks, also conveyed messages to every nerve ending in her body, setting her aquiver. How was it possible to feel so pleasantly languid and so urgently excited at the same time?

Was it only her imagination, because her own system

was out of sync, that *his* breathing seemed faster, too? He avoided looking into her eyes, appearing to concentrate solely on his self-assigned task. He didn't stop until he had coaxed every muscle in her calf into utter relaxation. He had a very persuasive touch, Niera reflected.

"Better?" he asked in a voice that sounded even huskier than it had earlier.

"Wonderful." Her reply slipped out on a long sigh.

"The water should be warm. It won't be as effective as a whirlpool, but I'm sure it will help you relax. Why don't you dangle your legs in the sea for a while?"

"Okay," she agreed quickly. Anything to put a little distance between them while she could still resist the urge to stroke his cheek, to feel the muscles of his shoulder beneath her arm again.

The distancing wasn't immediate enough. Instead, he began unhooking one of her sandals. She was experiencing feelings so primitive that she'd almost forgotten she was wearing shoes. His fingertips brushed her instep, and his thumbs trailed a caress along the sole of her foot as he removed each sandal.

She didn't realize what he intended to do until he began kicking off his own sandals. "Never mind," she stammered out. "I can get from here to the water by myself."

"No need to," he said, once again sweeping her up in his arms.

All the sensations she'd experienced the first time he carried her were magnified and multiplied now. She forced herself to remain rigid in his arms, holding herself away from his body as much as possible, merely resting a balancing hand on his shoulder.

He waded several feet into the water and deposited her gently on the overhanging palm trunk. The fallen tree shifted slightly under her weight, and he tightened his hold. His sudden embrace, intended to steady her, couldn't possibly have made her more unsteady. It must have been at that same instant, she told herself later, that she locked her arms around his neck.

She thought she sensed the vibration of his heart pounding in an accelerated pace with hers.

His aquamarine eyes locked with hers, and she was aswirl in drowning sensations that had nothing to do with the lagoon.

"Niera," he murmured, just before he joined his lips to hers.

They savored each other for a long moment, then relaxed even more as his tongue moved along her lips. She opened her mouth to him, and their tongues tenderly tangled together, exploring, pleasuring.

She felt his smile in his upcurving lips before she saw it. "You taste like coconut ice cream," he said, as if that was the world's most-sought-after treat.

"The flavor is mutual," she replied, matching his smile.

It was he who first pulled away, slowly. Niera's reaction to that was mixed: For once, it hadn't been she who pulled back first. Yet such a triumph was of questionable value.

He stared down into the water, kicking up a tiny tornado of sand with his toe and jamming his hands into his pockets as if to restrain himself from touching her. "I'm sorry," he murmured.

"Then I guess I should be sorry, too."

He gave a slight shrug of his marvelous shoulders. "I didn't mean to—"

"To take advantage of a gimpy lady?" she supplied wryly. "Don't worry. You didn't."

"I hope I didn't ruin our day."

"My day's intact," she responded lightly, without adding that her mind and emotions were in shambles, not to mention her out-of-control physical responses. "How's yours?"

"Terrific." He aimed a slight grin in her direction. "You rest there as long as you want, and I'll go window-shopping without the windows."

Niera was left dangling in more ways than one, she mused. But the water surrounding her legs did provide a satiny, soothing warmth.

Belatedly, it occurred to her to wonder whether coconut ice cream could override the taste of licorice and cigarettes. Their kissing had resulted in some additional information: This afternoon at least, Cort was strictly a one-flavor man.

She allowed herself the luxury of gazing at him on a prolonged basis while he wandered about the gigantic, airborne patchwork quilt of *pareos*. A couple of times, he glanced in her direction and waved.

He actually purchased several *pareos* in assorted colors and patterns. Keeping up the pretense? she wondered.

Eventually, he approached a display of *pareos* staffed by two young Tahitian women. Very pretty women, Niera noted with a slight frown. Cort bought as many *pareos* from this pair as he'd acquired from all the other vendors combined.

Still, he wasn't through. Apparently, she'd already been replaced as his future model, and that stung her ego even though he'd been kidding when he offered her the job—and even though these new models possessed special qualifications.

The women were demonstrating some of the myriad methods and styles of wrapping a *pareo*. Niera suspected that Cort's appreciative observation wasn't strictly for educational purposes.

She watched, too, trying to master the art of tying a knot over one shoulder, draping the fabric around the body, and tucking the end into the fold above the breasts.

These ladies sported very nice breasts, Niera couldn't

help noticing. And if she noticed, surely Cort did, too. The girls, with their honey-colored skin, flowing black hair, and liquid brown eyes, posed and postured, laughing and chattering. Although Niera was too far away to hear their words, she knew they were flirting with Cort. And he appeared to be responding with the enthusiasm of any red-blooded American male set loose in uninhibited, sensual Tahiti.

She gave the water a good swift kick. Maybe she could benefit from the ongoing lesson in coquetry, but she wasn't going to sit still for it anymore. Besides, staying inactive too long might cause her leg to stiffen up again.

She slipped off the palm trunk, only to find that the water was deep enough to soak the edge of her shorts—a fact they hadn't considered when taller Cort had waded out here with her in his arms.

She wouldn't worry about getting wet, she decided. Ignoring Cort and his two willing instructors, she strolled among the lines of *pareos*. She was selecting one from those offered by the amply proportioned mother of two children when a deep voice rumbled in her ear.

"Your leg's all right now?"

"Yes, thank you," she replied without turning around.

"I already bought one for you."

She turned to see him searching through the stack of *pareos* draped over his arm.

"It reminded me of a Tahitian sunset," he said. "At least it would if I'd ever seen one. Yesterday evening it was raining."

"Maybe tonight," she remarked as conversational filler.

"Maybe tonight," he repeated softly. "Anyway, I thought these colors would complement your hair and your tan."

Those aquamarine eyes were melting her. Were those eyes really, totally his? Niera wondered, to divert herself from becoming lost in them again. She couldn't exactly say, "Do you mind if I run my fingers over your bare eyeballs?"

She stopped staring into his eyes in search of contact lenses. She was becoming too easily distracted from her purpose.

He pulled out the *pareo* he'd chosen for her. It was a blend of oranges and yellows, the hues of sunset.

"Like it?" Cort asked.

"It's lovely," she said with a catch in her voice. "But I insist on reimbursing you for it. You must have bought it thinking that I couldn't get around on my own."

"Not at all. I wanted to get a gift for you."

"Thank you, but Mother told me never to accept presents from strangers."

"Not applicable in this case."

She drew a deep breath of expectation.

"See?" He found and tilted up the tiny label on one end. "One hundred percent cotton. Not mink, or even muskrat."

She couldn't help laughing. The *pareos* weren't expensive, only the equivalent of ten to twenty U.S. dollars. Overpriced maybe, but not expensive in terms of the world economy.

Pay your own way, stay your own woman, was another of Niera's personal mottoes. Quickly reviewing her personal mommyisms, she decided that one hadn't come from her esteemed parent. In fact, she seemed to recall something to the effect that marrying a rich man should be her primary goal.

With a smile, Niera agreed to accept the beautiful *pareo*. Then Cort noticed her damp shorts and was excessively apologetic about carrying her out too far.

She had gotten carried away earlier, in more ways than one, Niera mused. And she might get into really deep water, if she remained in his company much longer.

Cort returned to his private wrapping and tying demonstration while she purchased two other *pareos* for herself, plus a couple for her aunt and cousin. She bought a colorful print shirt for John. Then she took closer notice of one of the male vendors. She'd almost forgotten that men wore *pareos*, too, wrapped so as to leave their chests and legs bare. On a whim, she bought one in swirls of blue and green for Cort.

He didn't quite comprehend when she presented it to him. Then shock crossed his features while the Tahitian girls giggled.

"Getting even for getting slightly dunked?" His low tone was meant only for her ears. "You don't really expect me to wear that thing? On men, it looks like a skirt from the front and an oversized diaper from the back."

She shrugged. "Suit yourself, but I'm told *pareos* are cool and comfortable for men, too, in this humid climate."

The corner of his mouth quirked skeptically.

"Besides," she continued, "you're overlooking a whole potential market. Men might not buy these for themselves, but women might purchase them in pairs, one for themselves and the other for their men to wear at home or in their own backyards."

"Maybe you're right," he acknowledged with a sigh. "Some people will buy anything." That now-familiar smile blazed across his face again. "Let me work up to it, though. Don't make me wear it this afternoon."

"You don't have to wear it ever if you don't want to. Just consider it a souvenir gift from a fellow traveler."

"So that's it. You weren't getting even, just making sure to keep even."

The accuracy of that insight into her character was unsettling to Niera.

But she hadn't gotten even with him yet, Niera thought, with a sly glance at the lissome Tahitians. Using her damp shorts as an excuse, she concealed herself within the thick fringe of jungle edging the cleared area and changed into one of the *pareos* she'd bought for herself.

Cort was still chatting with the Tahitian girls when she returned and tapped him on the shoulder. She was rewarded with his sharp intake of breath when he turned and saw her.

Lavenders and violets streaked through her cotton *pareo*. Since she still had to bicycle back to the pier, she had forgone the most daring styles and settled for tying the top like a halter and swirling the fabric around. The *pareo* ended above her knees, and one tanned thigh peeked through the slit when she moved.

"You look wonderful," he murmured, unable to take his eyes off her.

"Just a little something I threw on," she replied honestly.

"I did some asking around. One of the vendors here has a car. I arranged for him to close down early, tie your bicycle on the back, and drive you to the pier in time to board the ship."

"I don't want to risk missing the boat," Niera said, with a secret double meaning. No way did she intend to let Cort Tucker out of her sight until she was sure he was safely aboard when the ship sailed tonight. "The vendor might get tied up with a late customer. Tahitians don't pay much attention to little things like time schedules. I'm fine now."

"I don't know—"

"The treatment was a success," she assured him in a soft voice.

"Maybe I should have been a physical therapist."

Maybe you are, she commented to herself, remembering his kiss at the lagoon. Aloud, they continued the discussion of her fitness to proceed. They argued for so long that she began to wonder whether he had her welfare in mind or whether he simply wanted to be free of her. Normally, she would have considered her company unwelcome and bowed out. But Niera Pascotti always got her man professionally, if not personally. And she wasn't through with this one yet.

"Okay," he relented finally. "I'll let you cycle back if we stop frequently and if you promise to let me know at the slightest twinge of pain."

"Agreed," she said. Her goal was to stay with him until they both sailed with the cruise.

They loaded their bicycle baskets with their purchases and her other clothing, then rode on.

She couldn't hold back an amused smile, noticing how often he glanced at her left leg. With each rotation of the pedal, her thigh flashed enticingly through the opening in her *pareo,* only to disappear again. Finally, it seemed he couldn't stop staring.

He glanced up to see her watching him. Guilty as charged, proclaimed the sheepish expression on his face. "I, uh, was just wondering how your leg is doing."

"Very well, thank you," she replied. Very well at achieving the desired effect, if his slightly glazed eyes were any indication.

They both looked away at the passing scenery. Then their eyes met again, and they burst into a duet of laughter.

He did insist on stopping frequently, and she enjoyed every interval. They dawdled at picturesque coves. They watched hollowed-out coconut husks moving up a conveyor belt to fuel the steam generator that provided much of Bora Bora's electricity.

Later, Cort consulted his guidebook and pointed out two circular thatch-roofed structures perched on stilts over the lagoon. "Those are Marlon Brando's and Jack

Nicholson's condominiums. Not far from here is the modest house where Brando's Tahitian wife, Tarita, was born."

He had been very solicitous throughout the afternoon. She refused to admit how very tired she was by the time they arrived at the tiny island capital.

They arranged to meet at the end of the pier to catch the tender to the ship hovering offshore. Then they discovered, chuckling together, that they had separately tempted fate that morning by renting their bikes from a man named Alfredo Doom.

She might be challenging destiny in more ways than that during the next few days, Niera realized. But she was feeling a hundred percent alive and vital for the first time in months. Was that because she liked the chase? Or the company of this man? Or were those two allurements intertwined?

If they boarded the ship now, she realized, he would have time to return to the island before sailing. At Niera's instigation, they dallied around the dozen mini-buildings nearby, passing up the Bora-Bora-Burger stand.

"There sure isn't much to do here," Cort remarked.

"Bora Bora would become boring-boring in a very short while, I suppose."

"With the right person, no place is ever boring." His fingertips brushed her arm, but she didn't meet his gaze.

Was he Mr. Right, Mr. Wrong, or Mr. Nonexistent? All she knew was that she felt a warm pleasure in just being with him, not to mention the zinging excitement of his touch.

He hadn't smoked all day, she reflected, and Royce would never have been able to quit with no visible pangs. Also, Royce was highly allergic, but Cort hadn't sneezed once. Of course, Hawaii might have some pollens not necessarily indigenous to Bora Bora, she admitted. Besides, moisture from the recent heavy rains would be holding down the pollens. Or perhaps Royce's allergies had abated if he'd quit smoking.

He broke into her tumultuous thoughts.

"Hey, I just remembered something," he said. "The name of this town, Viatape, means waterfall. But I didn't see any waterfalls coming or going. Did you?"

"No." She turned to stare at him directly. "Imagine that. Another genuine phony."

He abruptly averted his eyes, and the smile faded from his face. He jammed his hands into his pockets again in that unconscious shuttering gesture. He neither parried nor asked her to explain her comment. After one of the loudest silences she'd ever heard, he simply mumbled, "We'd better get back to the pier or we'll miss the last tender."

Chapter 4

BALANCING HERSELF AGAINST the mild sway of the ship, Niera descended the outside steel stairs. Bora Bora was receding in the distance. A small boat was heading away from the ship toward the island.

Briefly, she wondered whether Cort might be on that boat. Just because they'd boarded the ship together didn't mean he couldn't figure out a creative way to leave again.

He hadn't initiated any further plans with her. He hadn't even asked whether she was scheduled for the first or second seating at dinner, let alone suggested that they alter arrangements so they could be at the same table. After her "genuine phony" remark, he had made trivial chit-chat with other passengers on the pier and on the tender back to the ship, not excluding her, but not conversing directly with her, either.

Now she was making her way from the radio room back to her stateroom. The call she'd placed to Denver telephone information had confirmed what she'd expected: There was a listing for Dressed for Excess, but no one answered the telephone. Of course, it *was* Friday night in Denver, well after business hours. And since there was no answering service, she wouldn't be able to reach the company on Saturday or Sunday, either.

She couldn't call any of her colleagues. If the FBI had sent Royce or another agent, no one would admit it. And if they hadn't, her superiors would assume that her imagination was running amok and that she was psychologically unfit to be reinstated. So she was strictly on her own.

She went to the lounge to meet her friend. Freshly sunburned and smiling, Megan was seated at a table with several new friends of varying ages from the tour group she'd been with all day. She invited Niera to join them, but Niera declined. They determined that Megan had the first seating for dinner, while Niera was scheduled for the second seating.

Niera was eager to share her news of Royce with Megan, but she hesitated to burden Megan or distract her from the good time she was having. They agreed to meet for an early breakfast the next day, and Niera decided to tell her then.

Stopping at the purser's office, Niera verified that a Cort Tucker was in stateroom 140. Was it a coincidence that his room was on the same deck as hers, just a short way down the hall?

There was no point in searching his stateroom or picking his pocket. His passport would have to match the name on his cruise ticket. She had no doubt that any identification in his possession would appear to be authentic.

Questions begging for answers repeatedly assaulted Niera as she showered and styled her hair into soft fullness. She was going to enjoy this evening, and this cruise, she vowed. She'd be back on the case soon enough; a few additional days wouldn't matter after three months.

Niera made certain that she was among the first passengers to enter the dining room for the second seating for dinner, only to learn that her table was so far away from the door that she couldn't see whether Cort came in. Dinner was a blend of pleasant food and cordial talk with her tablemates, who represented an assortment of occupations and a geographical range of home locations in the United States.

The only discordant notes were sounded by Dr. Van Drexel, who wore a tuxedo, and his wife, who was decked out in a violet sequined evening dress in contrast to the more casual attire of the other tourists. Mrs. Van Drexel's eyes glinted with daggers rather than sequins as she glared over Niera's shoulder, muttering loudly, "What do you suppose it takes to be invited to the captain's table?"

"Now, dear, it's only our second night out," her husband replied. "I'm sure we'll receive an invitation eventually. If not, I'll certainly speak to the *maître d'*. Perhaps they've got *Mister* instead of *Doctor* in front of my name."

"*Our* names, dear."

Niera stifled a smile, concentrating on the baked Alaska, which seemed out of place in the South Pacific. Later, she allowed herself a mildly curious glance backward toward the captain's table, which was in the middle of the huge dining room.

She grew as rigid as the Van Drexels had been. Seated next to the captain was Cort, as attractive in a suit as he was in shorts.

Of course, she reasoned, the ship's staff would have no way of checking whether he was the corporate president he claimed to be. They'd no doubt take the word of a passenger who appeared to be important. The FBI wouldn't even have had to make any special arrangements.

The select eight passengers dining at the captain's table were in the midst of raucous laughter. Niera rose and left without attracting Cort's attention.

Walking along the deck, she became mesmerized by the utter darkness of the South Pacific. A halo of vagrant moonlight escaped from behind billowy black clouds, but the stars could not peek through. She chose a lounge chair in an isolated corner of the deck, but still she couldn't avoid the ebb and flow of loving couples aged twenty to eighty.

Eventually, another lone figure emerged from amid the pairs. Through half-closed eyes, Niera watched his uncertain approach until he was near enough to identify her with the help of the deck lights.

"There you are." Cort's deep voice washed over her. "I've been looking all over for you."

"Really," she said in her most apathetic manner.

"I'd already accepted the invitation to dine at the captain's table tonight before I knew you'd be on the cruise."

She restrained herself from reacting visibly to his choice of words. He hadn't said "before we met," but "before I knew you were on the cruise." The two phrases were not synonymous.

"Buy you a nightcap?" he offered.

"All right," she accepted. "I'd like a mixed drink: Coke with Coke Classic. The new blended with the old always makes an interesting combination."

"Any personality connection?" His question sounded only half kidding, and for an instant she thought he might reveal the truth. Then she realized he was referring to her personality rather than his own when he continued, "The old-fashioned girl blended with the new liberated woman?"

His description was more accurate than she cared to

admit. She deflected his question by joking, "I hope your advertising campaigns are more sophisticated, Tucker. Women would rather be compared to fine wine that improves with age or to sparkling champagne than to soda pop."

"I was thinking of you as effervescent and bubbly," he defended himself with mock gallantry before leaving for the bar.

Returning several minutes later, he handed her a glass. "Choices on this ship are limited. Only new Coke is available."

The nightclub show had just ended, and people were spilling onto the deck, surrounding Niera and Cort so that they had no opportunity for private conversation.

Finishing her Coke and checking her watch, Niera said, "It's nearly midnight. I want to get an early start after we dock at Raiatéa tomorrow. There's a lot to see."

"I was hoping we could see it together." After a moment's hesitation, Cort added, almost shyly, "I enjoyed our afternoon together."

"So did I," she replied honestly.

"Meet you at the bottom of the gangplank at eight?"

"It's a date." Even as she spoke, Niera wondered whether he considered it a social date or a business appointment with a suspect.

The next morning at breakfast, Niera's thoughts and feelings were as scrambled as the eggs on her plate as she told Megan about the events of the previous day.

"He hasn't done or said anything that would confirm he's Royce?" Megan asked when Niera had finished.

"No, but Royce is an agent, experienced at camouflage and game playing."

"Couldn't Cort Tucker be just who he says?"

Niera's croissant crumbled into as many directions as there were possibilities. "That's remotely possible. But it would be a big coincidence."

Megan sighed. "Coincidences do happen."

"Yes, but rarely," Niera observed. Her gaze turned dreamy.

"That night, Royce said he loved me. Maybe he's here now to prove it. That sizzle whenever he touches me isn't entirely from the tropical sun."

"But you never loved Royce," Megan reminded her gently.

"Maybe I would have if we'd had longer together. Or if I hadn't held back so much of myself. All I know is that I feel differently now. I'm tired of risking my life on the job and overprotecting myself in my personal relationships. I'm taking a chance on believing Royce is here because he cares about me. I've played a lot of roles on a lot of life's stages to suit the needs of other people. This one's for me. For the next week or so, I can play the part of a woman enjoying the company of a man she's just met on a cruise. I'm living in the present."

"But you're not," Megan blurted out her concern. "You're tangling it up in the past. Don't you see that as long as you believe he's Royce and that he isn't being honest with you, you can't become seriously involved? You're still protecting yourself."

"Am I? I feel at risk, just thinking of being with him again. I know I could be hurt. But if Royce's presence here is related to the case, I need to find out what he's up to. And if it's personal, I need to know that, too."

"I wish I could figure out some way to help you," Megan said sympathetically.

"You want to hear some more possibilities?" Niera asked, slugging down a large dose of orange juice as if it were stronger stuff. "If he truly is Cort Tucker and owns a clothing company, he could be here to see if I'll offer to sell him counterfeit merchandise, since I was suspected of complicity. Or he could be one of the criminals, checking me out."

Megan groaned. "But don't forget, he *could* be genuine, and not a phony at all."

"Well, it's multiple choice. I choose to believe that he's Royce, and I choose to go sight-seeing with him today."

Another glance at her watch confirmed that it was 8:35 A.M. She'd give Cort just five more minutes, Niera decided, ignoring the fact that she'd made that same decision five minutes earlier. Her future was ticking away while she waited for her present to show up.

She forced herself not to stare constantly at the stream of passengers flowing down the gangplank. Raiatéa, with the second largest port, was the only island in French Polynesia besides Tahiti where the ship could moor at the dock instead of remaining offshore.

The day was more polite than Cort Tucker, she mused. It was prompt in offering warm sunshine and azure skies with no threat of rain. Dressed in yellow shorts and a yellow striped top, she pretended her pacing had a purpose, browsing among the vendors' stalls that lined the neat, parklike waterfront.

A barefoot little girl walked up to her with a basket of flowers. Her blue eyes, black hair, and amber skin were a reminder of the ethnic blendings of French Polynesia. She selected and held out a huge scarlet hibiscus. *"Pour vous."*

Niera couldn't refuse. *"Merci."* She accepted the blossom, handing the little girl the equivalent of two dollars in local coins.

A wizened elderly woman with gray hair approached, smiling. The child's grandmother, Niera assumed. Reaching out a bony finger, she touched Niera's left ear, saying, "Looking." Then she touched the other ear. "Taken."

Niera understood that she was explaining the code of the flowers. Wearing a blossom over the left ear meant you were available and looking for a mate. Over the right ear meant that you were married or otherwise unavailable. It was a colorful, fragrant semaphore, visible from a far greater distance than a wedding ring.

She certainly wasn't taken, and she wouldn't admit to actively searching. Retrieving a bobby pin from her purse, she attached the flower in the center of her hair at the back, and resumed her stroll along the short waterfront.

A murmur in Tahitian began behind her, then grew in volume. Male voices chattered and giggled. She turned to see four Tahitian youths grinning good-naturedly while pointing at her and jabbing each other in that universal spirit of the male group leer.

"What—" she began, when Cort's voice interrupted from behind.

"I see you've acquired an entourage."

She turned to see that he was grinning, too. So much for the stalwart hero ready to defend her honor.

He fought the battle for her virtue not with a sword but with a hibiscus. He slipped the blossom out of her hair, shaking his head at her new followers. Still gawking occasionally and exchanging comradely chuckles, the boys dispersed.

"You did miss something in the guidebook," Cort told her, chuckling. "A flower worn at the back of the head means 'follow me.'"

"Well, maybe that's exactly what I intended," she teased smoothly.

"Sorry," he said, not the least bit abashed. "Your date was with me."

"*Was* is the proper tense." She tried not to notice how attractive he was in pastel green shorts and a green island print shirt. She didn't recall Royce's ever wearing anything other than somber colors. "You're forty-five minutes late."

"Not by Tahitian time. You wouldn't believe how

long it takes to arrange things around here. I hope you're not going to let a measly three-quarters of an hour persuade you to stand me up after all I've been through."

"I suppose I could let you explain, and then decide." Her lips hinted at a smile.

"I'll spare you the details of the hassles, if it's enough to say that I've rented an outrigger for now and a motor scooter for later."

It could take quite a while to arrange anything in laid-back Tahiti. "It's not exactly an offer of an air-conditioned limousine, but I guess it will do."

"Think of the motor scooter as a sleek convertible, and the outrigger as a mini-yacht."

He escorted her to the far end of the waterfront, where a small outrigger awaited. Only when he started to help her get in did they realize he was still holding her hibiscus.

The question in his eyes was reflected in hers while they both looked as panicked as two thirteen-year-olds at their first school dance. Left ear or right ear? Available or unavailable?

Drat, this flower code was complicated and required some rapid decisions, Niera mused. What was appropriate for a second date?

Cort held the blossom uncertainly between his thumb and forefinger, as their eyes met again and held.

Uncomfortable at her own responses to his nearness, she broke the spell by joking, "Maybe I should hold it between my teeth, like a flamenco dancer."

"That's the code for 'I'm hungry.'"

In his company, she did feel a strange hunger gnawing deep within her, Niera admitted. She was glad to be interrupted by the same pair of flower sellers, the girl and her grandmother. Young and elderly. New and old.

The woman reached into her loose bouquet and held

out a red hibiscus to Cort. "For you. For men, flower is closed or only part open."

How appropriate, Niera thought with a trace of bitterness. Closed or only partly open was certainly fitting. The woman didn't comment on the fact that her selection for him also was a different species of hibiscus—the one with multiple blooms instead of a single flower.

"Married?" The woman's question bounced between them.

"No," they both blurted out at the same time.

"Not married, then available," the woman said succinctly, placing the new hibiscus behind Cort's left ear. She grinned, showing yellowed teeth. "Sometimes available anyway."

How nice to have it simplified. Retrieving her own flower from Cort, Niera said with a shrug, "Unmarried is unmarried." She anchored the hibiscus behind her left ear.

Minutes later, they were skimming across the glittering turquoise water, facing each other as Cort manned the motor and steered.

A sudden puff of wind yanked the hibiscus away from her ear and flung it into the water. It floated there, bright but lonely and misplaced in the midst of the blue sea.

Not available. Perhaps the Polynesian gods had proclaimed that. Not emotionally available.

Cort had seen the flower blow away. Recognizing sympathy on his face, Niera realized that her own features must have looked more distressed then she'd intended, but she couldn't explain that she'd been thinking of more than the accidental loss of a flower.

"We'll get you another," he said softly. "That first one just wasn't meant for you."

They passed between the high, jungled slopes of Raiatéa and the *motus*—tiny, palm-studded coral islets —that dotted the lagoon.

Rounding the curve of the shore, Cort pointed the outrigger into a narrow channel. "This may be my only chance to send you up the river," he said.

"What?"

"The Faaroa," he continued, as if innocent of a double entendre. "It's the only navigable river in French Polynesia, so I thought we should explore it."

As they slowed, the lower murmur of the motor was more conducive to conversation.

"I was disappointed," Niera confided, "to learn that outriggers are now metal and motorized."

"Horrors. Don't tell me you would have expected me to paddle this far in a carved-out tree trunk."

"It would have a certain panache." She tried to divert her mind from a rugged image of Cort with bare legs and naked back, muscles shiny with perspiration and rippling in the sunlight.

"Maybe something more lavish would have suited you. Say, a galley on the Nile, propelled by a couple of hundred slaves."

Although relishing his comparison between herself and Cleopatra, she said, "I don't have expensive tastes."

"Don't you?"

"That constant drum pounding would have given me a migraine. How often do you suppose Cleopatra honestly said, 'Not tonight, Antony. I have a headache'?"

He laughed. "The rigors of royalty. So difficult to keep one's slaves working in the appropriate rhythm."

"At least in Tahiti, the drums change pace now and then."

Increasingly awed by the scenery around her, she remarked on a sigh, "This is just my speed. Absolutely perfect."

"Absolutely," he murmured so softly that she wasn't certain she'd heard it.

They were drifting through a leafy tunnel of vibrant green. Arching branches of trees from both riverbanks formed a verdant canopy above them, duplicated by reflection on the opalescent water.

As if by mutual accord, they enjoyed the primeval silence for several minutes, not feeling compelled to make conversation.

"I guess we're not the first human beings ever to pass this way after all," Cort said finally, as they passed a fishing net draped from a branch.

Eventually, the river became too narrow for passage, so they simply floated in the midst of the benign jungle.

Niera hated shattering the spell, but she knew she had to question him, and try to ascertain if he was Royce. She'd be equally interested in his answers if he was exactly what he seemed to be—an attractive stranger in a lulling paradise.

"Tell me more about yourself," she forced herself to say. "How did you get interested in the clothing business?"

"With four sisters—three older, one younger—I found it impossible to grow up without understanding the earthshaking importance of women's clothing," Cort said, chuckling. "While I majored in marketing at the University of Colorado, I moved through the salesclerk, buying, and assistant manager ranks at a local department store. Later, I became a manufacturer's representative for several clothing lines. My entrepreneurial streak eventually led me to start an independent clothing distribution and sales company, oversee some designing and manufacturing of my own, and sell other lines as well."

"And it's a good way to meet women," Niera teased, annoyed at the truth of that comment.

"It is. But I never mix business with pleasure."

If only everything he was telling her was true, and if only she could know for certain that she was his pleasure rather than his business.

"What are your sisters like?"

To her amazement, he answered in detail. He ex-

plained that the three oldest were actually half sisters
from his mother's first marriage. A few years after their
father died, she and Cort's father were married and had
two children together—Cort and his younger sister.

He seemed truly fond of his family, dropping into the
conversation all four sisters' names, their husbands'
names, their occupations, tidbits about assorted nieces
and nephews—even a mention of the dog he'd had
when he was young. And he talked about his current
roommate—a black and white Sheltie named Ramby,
short for Rambunctious.

Niera mentally filed all the details. It would be
highly unusual for an agent to volunteer any more information than absolutely necessary, no matter how thoroughly the cover story had been planned and
memorized. The less said, the less possibility for making a future mistake by not having all the facts coincide.

She would be delighted if Cort proved to be precisely
what he represented himself to be—a successful businessman making the most of a cruise. As soon as she
acknowledged that she wanted Cort to be what he
seemed, guilt pricked at her, since that would mean he
couldn't be Royce. And if he wasn't Royce, she must
accept that Royce, her partner, had died three months
ago . . .

"I've been rambling on far too long about myself,"
he said finally. "You're too easy to talk to."

"I'm not tired of hearing about you," she replied
honestly.

"I'm glad," he murmured, tracing her cheek with his
finger. "But it's your turn. How do you like living in
Honolulu?"

She feigned casualness as she said, "Honolulu? I
only told you that I live in Hawaii."

He looked away. "I guess I just assumed Honolulu,
since that's the only major city."

"You assumed right," she said. It was an understandable assumption, wasn't it? She proceeded to tell him mostly tourist-type information about Honolulu and very little about herself or her family. And she certainly didn't mention that she worked for the FBI.

She didn't want to actually lie to him, though. She tried to convince herself that was because she was on vacation, and lying was part of the day-to-day grind of her job back home. Here, she simply held back most of the truth. Royce already knew certain facts about her, and he might slip up and reveal himself by mentioning things she hadn't told "Cort."

She hoped he was being as truthful as she was.

"We'd better start back," she said, when she had exhausted her supply of small talk.

Revving the engine, Cort declared, "Now Tahaa."

"That's the sort of sound you'd make if you were being tickled," she yelled over the motor noise, although she knew he was referring to the neighboring island of Tahaa.

"Want to try tickling me to find out for sure?" He wiggled his eyebrows in mock lechery.

She wouldn't admit aloud that the prospect was rather appealing. But she allowed herself to wonder what it would feel like to slip her hands beneath his shirt, caress the firm tanned skin, spread her fingers lightly over his ribs . . .

"I think you're getting a sunburn on top of that tan," Cort remarked, staring at her.

"I'm wearing a gallon of sunscreen." It was necessary at this latitude, no matter how well one tanned normally. Then Niera realized she wasn't sunburned at all—her mental image of Cort had brought a rise of color to her cheeks. Good grief, she hadn't blushed in years. FBI agents definitely did not blush; she was sure that was stated clearly somewhere in the field manual.

Niera and Cort dawdled longer than they'd intended on the attractive, less-developed island of Tahaa, and barely made it back to Raiatéa in time to claim the motor scooter Cort had reserved to make a quick tour of the island.

As she climbed on behind him, he asked, "By the way, are scooters supposed to stay on the right side of the road or the left?"

"I don't know."

They both puzzled over that problem before solving it in unison, "In Tahiti, everyone drives in the middle of the road."

As they laughed together, Cort said, "When in Rome..." He watched the traffic for a moment before heading toward the main highway. "Scooters to the right," he tossed back.

"Right. Got it."

Her hands rested lightly above his waist, but as they gathered speed, she had to clasp him tighter. She locked her arms around him, absorbing the warmth of his flesh through the thin fabric of his shirt. She was glad that the wind snatched away any murmur of her more rapid breathing. They moved as one being, swaying with the curves in the road, her breasts occasionally brushing against his back.

The more prosperous agricultural island of Raiatéa seemed downright bustling after Bora Bora and Tahaa, as they zoomed along the narrow but well-paved highway out of the capital of Uturoa.

Cort turned onto the twisting route leading to the top of Mount Tapioi. The road became a slender thread of rutted dirt, a serpentine zigzag up and around the lush hillside. The back of the motor scooter gyrated like the hips of a Tahitian dancer, and the upward grade was so steep in places that Niera felt she was indeed likely to slide off the back. She had no choice but to cling more tightly to Cort, wishing for a quart of superglue to make sure she didn't wind up in the dust while he roared on ahead.

The views were worth the discomfort. Thick jungle tumbled down the hillsides toward the neat town of Uturoa. Beyond the island, they could see the ship moored in the harbor amid the spectrum of blues of the lagoon. The vast Pacific lay beyond the barrier reef.

Where the road ended, they climbed the short distance to the pinnacle where they could see Tahaa and, farther away, Bora Bora.

"See that blue mound in the distance?" Cort said, pointing to the left. "That must be Maupiti, over a hundred miles away. It's the island that time forgot, or that chose to ignore time, because the residents opposed hotels and other development. I was told it's only visible from here ten days a year." Absorbed in the panorama, he had slipped his arm around her shoulders as he spoke, as if to share it all in even greater intimacy. His clasp tightened, drawing them nearer. "We must be having one of those lucky days."

Distant, forbidden Maupiti, where yesterday merged into today and tomorrow, shimmered across the sea. Niera almost expected it to disappear, like a mirage. It seemed a special dollop of magic on their horizon, as if time were standing still just for them.

She felt as if she had melded into Cort, as if their joined souls were wafting across that expanse of ocean to blend into a timeless future. "It looks almost mystical, as if it touches down to earth only once in a while, like Brigadoon." The soft wistfulness of her own voice surprised her.

The depth of her feelings in that moment alarmed her. She pulled away, beating a quick emotional retreat with a joke. "Sorry, wrong musical. There's no heather on the hills here."

He didn't try to hold her physically when she drew away, but his eyes held hers in a way she couldn't escape. "I wouldn't say Brigadoon was totally inappropriate in this particular moment in the South Pacific.

That show had a few fitting tunes." He trailed his fingertip along her cheek with exquisite tenderness. "'Almost like Being in Love' . . ." He traced her half-open lips. "'Come to Me, Bend to Me' . . ."

She stood there, mesmerized by her feelings, terrified by her feelings, as he caught her chin and gently tilted her face toward his. A recollection of her lone hibiscus floating on the water flashed into her mind. Not available. Not emotionally available.

But that wasn't true. She was aching with availability. And vulnerability. A new, raw, frightening vulnerability.

Before he could kiss her, she stepped away. "If *Brigadoon* is suitable to French Polynesia, I guess you'll have to sell tartan *pareos.*" She turned to go back down the slope, leaving inane prattle in her wake like a cloud of dust. "Think of the fashion shows you could present, accompanied by bagpipes and conch shells. And plaid *pareos* might someday replace kilts for Scotsmen . . ."

She stopped only when she arrived alongside at the motor scooter, sensing his presence close behind her.

"I suspect you're full of creative ideas, Ms. Niera Pascotti."

She saw that the smile in his voice was reflected on his lips as he passed in front of her to steady the motor scooter.

She was glad he couldn't see her face as they returned to town. If even ten percent of her feelings were on display as she clung to him, he might not let her escape so easily the next time.

The sun had begun its brilliant glide into night when they arrived at the beach for a *tamaaraa,* a traditional Tahitian feast.

"This is very similar to a luau," Niera explained to Cort, reminding herself that he might have firsthand knowledge of the Hawaiian feast. "Roast suckling pig cooked in a deep pit with hot stones, poi." She took another bite. "The breadfruit and baked bananas are an original touch, though."

"This isn't much of a contrast for you," Cort said. "Why did you pick French Polynesia?"

"Lots of reasons. Back to the basics. See where the Hawaiians originated. Terrific diving." She omitted mentioning her main reason for coming here—to get away from it all. That plan hadn't worked out so well.

After dining, they watched a reenactment of the ancient fire-walking ceremony, which had originated when it had been essential to walk across the hot stones in order to place food in the middle of gargantuan oven pits.

Now Tahitian men in traditional costume poked at the stones with long sticks. The fire below hissed, and occasionally a long tongue of flame licked out like a serpent sensing prey.

Niera and Cort coughed along with the rest of the audience as great clouds of smoke billowed into the night while the men wielded their poles, carefully arranging the scorching stones to form a flat surface with tight-fitting seams and no sharp edges.

At last, only thin curls of smoke found their wispy way to freedom, phantomlike reminders of the smoldering depths.

An elderly priest wearing blue jeans beneath his leaf skirt passed a sheaf of leaves around the edge of the fire pit, chanting incantations. When he was finished, he called forth the spirit of a woman, embodied in his wife, to make the first crossing. He and the other men walked across the pit only after groups of women had traversed it several times.

"Playing with fire," Niera murmured aloud, talking to herself more than to Cort. "Since ancient eras, the men get things all stirred up, put up a heavy smokescreen, then let the women take the biggest risk of being burned."

"Once in a while, a man can get burned, too," Cort mumbled in reply.

After they returned to the ship along with a large group of passengers, Niera declined his invitation for a nightcap. Her head was throbbing, overtaxed by this whole situation. A hangover tomorrow wouldn't help.

She found Megan gyrating in the ship's disco. Megan started to excuse herself to talk with Niera, but Niera explained that she had a headache and was going straight to bed. She mentioned to Megan only that she had no new revelations to report.

She dreamed of hibiscus blossoms, and burning coals . . . and Cort.

Chapter 5

JUST CRUISIN'. The phrase took on new meaning for Niera the next day. When she booked passage on the cruise, she'd complained about this one day of enforced relaxation at sea, knowing that she'd prefer to participate in local activities. The next island was only twenty-five miles away, so the ship was dawdling in deference to those who liked cruising for its own sake.

"I know why they named the deck game shuffleboard," Niera told Cort. "Because the ship's just shuffling along."

She and Cort spent the entire day together, beginning with breakfast. They had no privacy, but they did enjoy each other's company. When their paths crossed Megan's, Niera introduced her as a new friend who had stayed at the same hotel on Bora Bora. Megan, who was occupied with the same young group who patronized the disco, couldn't help staring, but Niera felt that Megan controlled herself well.

When Niera could keep her mind from wandering into all the emotional crannies where Cort's presence led it, she reluctantly made an effort to trip him up on the details of his life. She dropped a casual remark here, a brief comment there, designed to verify the facts he'd told her earlier. He never missed.

By evening, she was ready to relinquish her half-hearted testing. He'd taken a small child off a harried mother's hands and had engaged the girl in the Ping-Pong match she'd been begging for. While watching them, Niera reviewed the last three days.

He was going easy on the girl, letting her win. Now and then, he threw back his head and laughed at some childish joke.

Was it in that moment, or earlier in the day, or sometime in the past, that she realized this was the man she'd been waiting for all her life?

She admired his intelligence and quick wit, the business acumen she'd discerned. The way he could lose himself in another culture and derive genuine pleasure from simple things. Cort moved and acted with a confidence that could be born only of past success, yet he could reach out and tug at her heart with those vulnerable moments when he seemed shy or uncertain of something he wanted to say to her. He had the ability to take charge, yet he never tried to dominate her.

This was the man she'd been waiting for all her life.

But was he real? Or the fabrication of a skilled agent? A person with whom to spend a lifetime, or a wispy persona who could vanish in a twinkling once there was no further need for him?

Pulling herself out of her reverie, she glanced at her watch. Time to change for dinner. She wanted to look her best tonight.

She interrupted Cort between serves. "Meet you at dinner. I can't stand to watch you being slaughtered at Ping-Pong any longer."

"So you really do care?"

She answered him with a smile as she walked away. Then she turned back and gave him a wink.

Later, as she joined the crowd heading down the staircase to the dining room, the soft fabric of her long, backless coral dress whispered around her ankles. She was glad she'd succumbed to the urge to buy it before the cruise. It matched her favorite coral lipstick and nail polish. Tonight she'd even polished her toenails, visible in her strappy silver evening sandals.

In fact, all through her shower, her careful hair styling, a thoughtful makeup application that involved changing eyeshadow colors twice—the whole female routine that she usually considered boring—she had felt that interior tingle of excitement. She sensed that this was the ritualistic beginning of a very pleasant evening. She was vaguely reminded of what it had been like to be eighteen, but tonight held more promise.

Only when she entered the dining room did she remember that each dinner guest was assigned to a certain table. She and Cort would have to ask to be seated together.

Finding him in the last place she looked—at her original table—she assumed that he'd already arranged the change.

The expression on his face when he first saw her was an ample reward for the extra time she'd spent getting ready. He, too, appeared to have dressed for a special evening, in a lightweight white suit with an aqua silk shirt that enhanced the turquoise of his eyes.

"You two are awfully formal tonight," Mrs. Van Drexel commented as Cort pulled out Niera's chair. "Most of us are wearing *pareos* all the time now."

"I only hope they catch on as fast in the United States as they have on the ship," Cort remarked.

Indeed, even Mrs. Van Drexel had traded her sequined gown for a pair of *pareos,* wrapped top and bottom around her ample figure. Dr. Van Drexel, who had gone only half-native, was wearing a flowered shirt with his blue serge trousers.

"I felt like dressing up," Niera said with a shrug. As Cort guided her chair back in, his fingertips brushed one of her shoulders, bared by the halter top. Niera tingled with the knowledge that he couldn't resist touching her any more than she wanted him to resist.

The cheery waiter arrived to take their orders. "Mr. Tucker," he greeted Cort. "I've missed you at our table since the first night."

Niera was gripped by a chill that couldn't be attributed to the air conditioning. How far could coincidence stretch? She turned to Cort. "You were originally seated at this table?"

"Oh, yes," Mrs. Van Drexel piped up. "He was ever so charming our first night out from Tahiti."

So Cort hadn't switched the seating. They'd been assigned to the same table all along, but he'd been a guest at the captain's table on the second night, and they'd both dined on Raiatéa last night. Donning her warmest smile despite the chill pervading her, Niera turned her attention to Mrs. Van Drexel. "Well, I'm sorry I missed all that charm. What did he talk about?"

"Oh, he told us ever so many funny stories about the clothing business."

Dr. Van Drexel gave Niera a chummy elbow in the general area of the ribs. "Wouldn't talk about the sexy models, though." He emitted a coarse laugh. "Mustn't be the type to kiss and tell."

"Is that all he talked about?" Niera asked, gazing with fascination at Mrs. Van Drexel.

"Oh, let me think." She didn't really pause long enough for Cort or anyone else to get a word in. "He talked about his dog, his sisters—"

"He came to Tahiti to get some ideas on *pareos,* you

know," Dr. Van Drexel interrupted. "Let me tell you, the contents thereof are what give me ideas."

"Really, George." Those two words from his wife were a scalding rebuke.

"I'd think you'd get kind of tired of bodies in your business, *Doctor* Van Drexel," Niera remarked.

"What?" said Dr. Van Drexel. "Oh, I see. No, not really. Business never interferes with pleasure."

Niera picked at her food, more interested in digesting the new information. Had "Cort" practiced his cover story on his tablemates the first night, even though Niera hadn't been on the cruise yet?

They were halfway through the meal when a near tragedy erupted. A cry of alarm went up from the next table when Cort's little Ping-Pong partner from that afternoon began to choke violently. Cort and Niera both sprang out of their chairs, but he was closer.

He grabbed the little girl from behind in the "hug of life" and performed the Heimlich maneuver. A huge hunk of melon was ejected from the child's mouth.

"Oh, honey," her tearful mother said, gathering her daughter in a different type of hug, "I've warned you not to take such big bites."

The ship's doctor and other crew members had responded to the commotion, but Cort had gotten there ahead of all of them.

Almost unconsciously, he and Niera slipped their arms around each other as they returned to their own table.

"Quick response," she said sincerely. But she had to add, "Where did you get your training?"

"In a Red Cross first-aid course, same as most people, I guess. I've had everybody at my company take it."

And all FBI agents were trained in first aid, as Niera herself had been. Only when they were seated again did she register the fact that Dr. Van Drexel had not responded to the emergency at all.

The pall that hung over the balance of dinner was dispersed when the little girl, now completely recovered, bounced up to Cort halfway through dessert and challenged him to another game of Ping-Pong.

"It's probably a good idea to keep her mind off what happened," he whispered to Niera. "Meet you in the nightclub in half an hour or so?"

She nodded her agreement. After Cort left, she tried to get Dr. Van Drexel to tell her just what his medical specialty was, but he rushed away.

After waiting a bit for Cort in the ship's nightclub, Niera strolled out onto the deck to watch the ocean beneath the sprinkling of stars and to listen to the low music from inside. She almost believed she could walk across the silvery cape cast on the water by the pale moon.

The sweet scent of frangipani titillated her nose. Like that night near the pier in Honolulu—

No, there was nothing to be gained by dwelling on those memories. That was the past. Tonight was the present.

The fragrance grew stronger; it seemed to be emanating from behind her. She turned to see Cort holding a lei of creamy frangipani and red hibiscus.

She didn't want to shatter the mood, didn't want to think about anything except the man standing before her. But who was he?

In all the time they'd spent together, she hadn't heard him sneeze, nor had she seen any other allergic reaction to the tropical pollens. But medication could sometimes control allergies. Still, though, it had been a truckload of frangipani blossoms that had triggered Royce's allergy that night at the pier in Honolulu . . .

Niera forced herself to ask, "You're not allergic to flowers?"

Cort looked startled, then puzzled. Then a chuckle bubbled out of him. "Niera Pascotti, you say the most romantic things in the moonlight."

His dimpled smile almost made her forget her question, as he answered. "No, I'm not allergic to flowers or anything else. Are you?"

She had once been allergic to emotional involvement, but not anymore, she answered silently. She shook her head.

He lifted the flower necklace over her head. As he draped it over her shoulders, his fingers lingered on her sensitized bare skin.

"This should be perfect," he said softly, his smile supplanted by a serious expression. "It can't slip off, like a single flower. And you don't have to decide whether to wear it on the left or the right."

"It is perfect," she whispered as his eyes held hers in the moon-glow.

"May I have this dance?"

She answered by stepping into the open circle of his arms.

As his hand touched the naked skin of her back, a shiver raced through her, a long-drawn-out quiver that seemed to reverberate through him as he pulled her closer.

Oddly, it was his gift of flowers that kept them from totally melding together in that moment. He couldn't hold her tighter without crushing the delicate blossoms.

His hand began a small circular caress on her back, in tempo with the music reaching out to them like a melodic wraith floating on the breeze. Only with the greatest effort did they begin a semblance of a slow dance step in rhythm with the tune.

Our present's tense,
No future sense,
Tomorrow's no promise today.
But cling to me,
Closed eyes can't see
If love might slip away.

Maybe we can pretend things are
the way they ought to be,
If we don't subject each other
to such close scrutiny.

Vaguely, Niera recognized the song as a new tune
she'd heard only once or twice before. Even more
vaguely, she wondered whether Cort had specially requested it.

My presence here
Means something, dear.
Let tonight postpone tomorrow.
Hold back that tear,
Just hold me near;
The dark can blot out sorrow.

Maybe we can pretend we are
whoever we ought to be,
If we don't subject each other
to such close scrutiny.

The heady fragrance of the frangipani filled her nostrils, but Cort commanded all her other senses. She lost
herself to him while the plaintive lyrics echoed through
corridors of her mind.

Love can elude;
Life can intrude;
Tomorrow may be mere dreams,
Or the best may last

For future and past.
Maybe all is what it seems.

Maybe we can pretend all is
the way it ought to be,
If we don't subject each other
to such close scrutiny.

She lifted her face to the man who held her so thrill-
ingly in his arms. Once again, his gaze enveloped her so
that she wanted only to remain in this warm cocoon.

Maybe we can pretend all is
the way it ought to be . . .

"Isn't there," he said on breath as quick as her own,
"some sort of kissing custom with the presentation of a
lei?"

Her own breathing seemed suddenly suspended.
There was the night silvered by the moon, the phantom
refrain of a distant tune, and Cort, amid the permeating
sweetness of the frangipani.

Cort, leaning forward to touch his lips to her cheek,
drawing back ever so slightly before kissing her other
cheek.

Cort, and the heavy aroma of frangipani feathered
with a spicy-minty scent. The spicy-minty after shave
that she recalled inhaling in her hospital room before
she'd been fully conscious.

The static on the long-distance telephone connection
seemed to crackle through Niera, too. Now the time
difference between Tahiti and Denver worked in her
favor, since Monday morning business hours began
there before the ship even anchored.

At last there was an answer on the other end.
"Dressed for Excess."

"May I speak with Cort Tucker, please? I'm calling
long-distance," Niera said.

"Mr. Tucker is out of the country on business," replied a woman's polite voice.

"Do you have a number where he can be reached?"

"He's not available for calls. May I take a message?"

"When will he return?"

"That's uncertain. In a few days, I believe. Could his assistant help you?"

"I'll call later in the week." Niera handed the telephone back to the ship's operator in the radio room.

As she'd suspected, she had no way of easily confirming from this distance whether Dressed for Excess really existed or whether the FBI had set up a switchboard to intercept calls to a fictitious company.

Cort had been bewildered last night when she'd stiffened in his arms and cut the evening short. But she had agreed to meet him early this morning to tour Huahiné. If only she could convince herself that she was eager for his company merely because she was intrigued by the unsolved mystery he presented.

She'd arranged to meet Cort on the pier, so she took the tender to shore alone.

It seemed Cort was always a step ahead of her. He was already waiting on the pier, wearing cream-colored twill shorts. His shirt was an abstract print of pinks from hot to pastel—very attractive on him, but a type that a less confident man might hesitate to wear.

With a grand sweep of his arm, he announced, "I am the temporary but proud possessor of one of the only five rental cars on Huahiné. And as if that weren't a coup in itself, I've also hired one of the few English-speaking guides available."

"I'm duly impressed." Niera matched his grin. "And the shirt's great, too." On second thought, she wondered if she could trust a man whose wardrobe was better than her own.

"Thanks. I like bright things. Bright colors." He

looked upward. "Bright sunlight." He looked at her. "Bright women."

Their Tahitian guide, Juli, also proved to be bright as well as beautiful. But Niera noticed time and time again, with a tingle of pleasure, that Cort seemed to have eyes only for her.

Juli kept up a running commentary, stopping at appropriate spots along the highways that circled the islands, for there were actually two Huahinés, joined by a short bridge.

"In Tahitian, *nui* means big, and *iti* means little, so you can tell which island is larger by the names—Huahiné-Nui and Huahiné-Iti," Juli said.

Cort had insisted that Niera share the front seat of the compact Peugeot with the guide, so she could see better. But he usually balanced on the edge of the back seat, leaning forward, to better catch the sights and the commentary. Often his and Niera's cheeks were close to brushing, but never quite did so. With a twist of her head, she could have joined her lips to his.

Their seating arrangement and Juli's presence left little opportunity for private conversation. But when they stopped and walked around a scenic spot, Cort loosely took her hand in his.

"Here are the missing waterfalls," Niera remarked, glimpsing the fluid silver through the thick jungle of Huahiné-Iti. The hillsides were a deep green velvet, with lakes and ponds nestled at their feet, fringed with flower-strewn beaches bordering the seaside lagoon. As on the other islands, the beaches were so narrow that one tall person could scarcely lie perpendicular to the water.

Stakes jutted out of one of the ponds. "This is an operation for cultivating black pearls, which has so far been successful only in French Polynesia because of the temperature and the other water conditions," Juli explained. "Black pearls are grown in the black-lipped oyster. The oyster is injected with a tiny granule, and defends itself by depositing layer upon layer of mica on the irritant. In the two years required for culturing a pearl, the oyster will coat that granule with more than six thousand layers of mica."

Something ugly and painful layered over again and again, so it appeared to be something beautiful. The lustrous and appealing black pearl was actually a disguised irritant. Niera couldn't help staring at Cort as those thoughts flickered through her mind.

"Less than ten percent of the harvested pearls are gem quality," Juli was saying, "and only one in three thousand is perfect."

Perfect. That was Cort. Her perfect man. One out of thousands. One in a lifetime.

And he might consist of nothing but layers of glossy camouflage.

Near the town of Maeva, they watched boys literally herd fish into watery corrals, where they were then scooped up in nets. Niera couldn't help wondering if she was being lured into a similar trap.

In another small settlement, Juli stopped by a stream and said something in Tahitian to three children who were playing nearby. They jumped into the stream with shrieks of laughter, gaily splashing the water.

Soon the stream was alive with the long, thick black bodies of eels arcing through the transparent water. "The eels love to come and play with the children," Juli said.

The two oldest children tried to grab the eels and lift them up for Cort and Niera to see more clearly. But they were cheerfully unsuccessful.

"I guess the expression 'slippery as an eel' has some basis in truth," Niera remarked.

During the day, they passed several *marae,* ancient

Polynesia temples made of black stones. Late in the afternoon, they stopped at one of the largest.

Facing the sea stood several curved black stones sculpted in the shape of cathedral arches about three feet high. Nearby was a stone platform—about the right size for an ancient production of *South Pacific,* Niera thought. Then Juli explained that it was once an altar for human sacrifice. Pale green lichen now grew over the black stones that had once run red with blood.

"The Polynesian king who ruled this island had a very strict law against trespassing," Juli told them. "Anyone who arrived without permission was immediately put to death."

"Swift justice," Niera murmured, as much to herself as to Cort. "I guess it had its advantages." Through her mind flashed some of the frustrations she'd had to deal with as an FBI agent.

"There was a time when I would have favored quick, sure justice," Cort murmured. "But now I can see how many times it might have gone awry."

Niera tried not to dwell on either his comments or her own. This was supposed to be her vacation, in the present. She didn't want to dwell on the past or face the future.

She wanted very much to hang on for the moment to the joy she usually felt in Cort's company, regardless of whether or not it was justified.

By the end of the day, her head was pounding with unanswered questions. And her heart pounded every time Cort touched her hand or beamed his smile in her direction.

Head and heart. Soon one would have to prevail over the other, Niera mused.

By the time they drove back toward the pier, clouds had gathered in the sky, blotting out the prospect of a spectacular sunset.

* * *

Niera met Megan at the deck bar at five o'clock and maneuvered her way through several minutes of small talk until she confirmed that Megan was enjoying the cruise and making new friends of various ages. Finally, Niera related her own recent adventures since they'd last talked.

"He's never tripped up," she concluded over her Mai Tai. "He's openly, easily, and thoroughly discussed his personal and professional life, both present and past. It would be very unusual for an agent to reveal so many details. And I've never been able to catch him in an inconsistency."

"So you finally accept that he really is Cort Tucker, and not Royce Taggart?" Megan asked.

"Sort of."

"*Sort of?* What does that mean?"

"I've figured out a whole new possibility," Niera said. "I still think Cort and Royce are one and the same man, but now I believe that Royce was the disguise."

"*What?*"

"Royce was much more guarded about his personal life and his feelings. I got to know less about him in a month than I've learned about Cort in a few days. The physical resemblance remains, but all the cosmetic components of Royce's disguise could have been faked. He could have grown a mustache, darkened his hair, worn light blue contact lenses, pretended to be addicted to cigarettes and licorice—he could even have faked the allergies by pretending to sneeze."

"But why would he do that?"

"He has expertise and contacts in the clothing business, so maybe the FBI recruited him to crack that particular smuggling operation. Maybe he's not free to explain that to me, even now."

"Then you believe he meant it when, as Royce, he

said he loved you? And he's here now because of that?"
Megan asked quietly, without enthusiasm.

"It could be." Niera's response lacked conviction.
"Almost anything could be in this topsy-turvy world."

"I guess so," Megan murmured, but she averted her
gaze.

"I suppose you're thinking that I'm still not accepting
Royce's death, that my new theory merely changes his
status from dead to nonexistent."

Megan sighed. "At least you've considered that possibility. Too bad you can't read Cort's mind as well as
you're reading mine."

She took another sip of her drink before commenting
further. "I hate to see you clinging to such a farfetched
theory. I have no answers, but I can't help pointing out
that there's nothing to connect Cort to Royce except
circumstantial evidence, as you legal types like to say.
Very circumstantial—just a certain physical resemblance."

"Maybe a little more."

"Intuition?" Megan asked.

"That, and bits and pieces. Hesitations in replying
sometimes, particularly on that first day on Bora Bora.
A flitting facial expression. An occasional remark that
doesn't click quite right, or could have a double meaning."

"Circumstantial in the extreme."

"I know." After a pause, Niera added with difficulty,
"You know there wasn't much physical evidence left to
sift through after the explosion. They did find a charred
piece of Royce's watch, which they identified by the
engraving on the back, and a couple of other things. But
there can't be solid evidence of a death in that type of
situation."

"Oh, Niera—" Megan said, with a sympathetic sigh.

"I know. We've been over this before. I feel so much
guilt over the death of my partner that I'd rather believe

he's alive." She leaned forward in the deck chair, feeling tense. "But there's still the silhouette I saw at the end of the pier before the explosion. At the time, I assumed it was a third person, but it could have been Royce. He could have survived somehow."

"Is there a possibility," Megan ventured softly, "that your having to be suspicious and analytical and untrusting in your career for so many years is coloring your judgment now?"

"I've asked myself that a thousand times," Niera admitted. "You can appropriately wrap one of those *pareos* around me straitjacket style if I keep this up much longer. Trying to figure out all the possibilities is driving me absolutely and irrevocably nuts."

"Do you prefer any particular color for your straitjacket?" Megan asked with a grin. Abruptly, her expression changed, and she exclaimed, "Cort could have made a deal with the FBI!" Pain flashed across Niera's face, and Megan belatedly said, "Oh, I'm sorry. I blurted that out without thinking how it might hurt you. I learned the hard way about the deals struck between criminals and the so-called justice system."

"It's okay. I thought of that, too. I just tried not to dwell on it," Niera murmured. She summarized what they were both thinking. "Cort could have been forced to disguise himself as Royce and work with the FBI because of some criminal involvement of his own. They could have agreed to let him off in exchange for his assistance."

"Oh, gosh. Straitjackets *are* destined to become the next fashion trend. I'm going to need one, too, if I keep trying to figure all this out. What are you going to do?"

"As soon as the cruise is over, I'm flying to Denver to check Cort's story. Then, with or without Hal's permission and the resources of the FBI, I'm going back to Honolulu to crack that smuggling operation."

"Will you let me come with you and help?"

"No. Absolutely not," Niera replied emphatically.

"I don't suppose there's any point in trying to change your mind?"

Niera shook her head slowly.

"With no special training or skills, I could be more of a burden and liability than a help. Just something else to worry about," Megan observed aloud.

"We've always been honest with each other. I can't tell you that's not true," Niera replied hesitantly. She didn't add that she wouldn't place Megan in danger under any circumstances.

"Then I'm going to stay at my cousin's in Topeka for a while after the cruise. But I'll hope for a call from you every night with an update."

"I'll call you as often as possible."

"What are you going to do during the next few days, until the cruise is over?" Megan prodded gently.

The setting sun bathed Niera's face in a golden glow —a fantasy glow. "I've decided to enjoy the rest of the cruise. This is my vacation from the past and from the future, remember? I've played lots of roles in my life, and I mean to play this one for me for all it's worth. I can write the script any way I want, so for the next few days, I choose to believe that Cort Tucker is exactly who he says he is, and nothing more or less." With an air of finality, she stood up. "And *que será, será,* even if this is the wrong part of the world for Spanish."

Niera started to leave, then turned back and asked, her imploring gaze probing Megan's eyes, "Am I really crazy? Am I doing the right thing?"

"The right thing," Megan replied, with sudden conviction, "is to grab on to happiness when you have the chance. Hold on to it if you can, but don't be so worried about keeping your hold on it that you fail to treasure every moment."

She took a deep breath before adding softly, "Even if I'd had Daniel for only one day instead of one year, our time together would have been worth a lifetime of grief and pain. I'd give anything if he were here now in any guise." The last sunlight shimmered on the sea, and on the dew of tears on Megan's cheeks. "But Daniel's not here. Cort, Royce, or whoever, is. So go for the happiness, Niera, and hold it for as long as you can."

Chapter 6

NIERA'S HEART DID triumph over her mind.

Or perhaps her heart had been surreptitiously aided by her mind, in her determination to savor the present while holding the past at bay a little longer.

Her awareness of Cort Tucker suffused her entire being.

She and Cort had spent all their time together for the past three days, but they had rarely been alone. Although these small islands didn't seem crowded even when the ship poured forth an extra eight hundred people for one day, it was difficult to find a spot that remained totally private for long.

They had joined a horseback-riding group on their second day on Huahiné, and had hiked through the jungle to still another waterfall with still another group of tourists. The next day was filled with on-board activities as the ship drifted through another full day at sea. Niera had felt as if she and Cort belonged together, like the couples surrounding them, most of whom had been married at least ten years, some more than forty years.

Last night, many of those couples had renewed their marriage vows in a touching ceremony. Watching, she and Cort had stood side by side, arms around each other, their gazes locking, then flicking away. Was he imagining, as she was, their repeating similar words?

She and Cort had dallied away today touring the island of Mooréa, only twelves miles from Tahiti, and snorkeling with Megan and a group of other passengers.

Niera stood under the shower in her stateroom now, pleasurably reviewing the last three days. As the spray rinsed away the last grains of sea salt from her skin, she tried to let go of any remaining residue of doubt about Cort.

Well, maybe not quite the last smidgen, she admitted. As soon as she returned to the United States, she still intended to check on Cort's identity, to quiet that nagging doubt.

But that could wait until the cruise was over. She still wasn't ready to think about the future. She was well aware that a shipboard romance was almost always fleeting. Niera had lived in the tropics long enough to have some immunity to the spell of the islands, and she knew that Cort might have succumbed to the awesome power of the setting rather than to her personal charms.

He had said nothing about seeing her after the cruise . . . yet she couldn't imagine never seeing him again.

As she smoothed lather over every inch of her nakedness, Niera longed for his touch. In her memory, she drifted back through the hours she'd spent in his tight embrace on the dance floor during the past two nights, when it seemed they were moving to a private, sublime rhythm despite the other couples dancing around them.

The vocalist must have been fond of that new song: "Close Scrutiny." She'd sung it both nights. Some of the lyrics were now ingrained in Niera's memory.

Maybe we can pretend all is
the way it ought to be,
If we don't subject each other
to such close scrutiny.

No more thinking. No more comparisons. No more
torturing herself with wondering. She and Cort had only
tonight and tomorrow before the return flight. And she
intended to make the most of it.

As she finished blow-drying her hair, there was a
knock on her cabin door. The steward handed her a
small box tied with yellow ribbon, with a lovely sea-
shell on top.

Cort Tucker's expertise with innovative packaging,
she hoped, eagerly opening it.

Inside was a lone creamy-white blossom that she recognized as a *tiare Tahiti,* a special type of gardenia
found only in French Polynesia.

She read the accompanying note: "Please meet me on
the dock in an hour. I'll show you my *pareo* if you'll
show me yours."

Donning the *pareo* he'd given her on Bora Bora,
Niera felt as if she were wrapping herself in the colors
of sunset, a reflection of her blazing feelings for Cort.
She arranged a soft fold of fabric above her breasts and
tied the garment over one shoulder, leaving the other
shoulder bare. Once again, her left thigh flashed
through the side slit.

She hesitated only an instant before fastening the
tiare Tahiti behind her left ear. "Unmarried is unmarried," she echoed the elderly lady on Raïatéa. Adding
another bobby pin, she continued the thought: Available
is available. The spicy gardenia fragrance would be a
continual reminder.

Once again, Cort was ahead of her on the dock. Had
it not been for his blond hair, she might have mistaken

him for one of the locals. His tan had deepened in the last week, and he was wearing the *pareo* she'd presented him on the day they'd met. His lower torso was a swirl of blues and greens, and the loose end of the cloth slanted downward midway to his outer thigh, in one of the popular male Tahitian styles. She noted that he'd passed up the equally popular style of simply tucking the *pareo* around his waist like a long skirt. Even that would not have lessened the impact of his powerful masculinity.

A tingle zipped through her as he took her arm to help her out of the tender.

"I didn't believe you'd really wear that," she said with a laugh.

"*You* look terrific. And it isn't nice to make fun of me."

"Who's making fun? You've got great legs." Her words were teasing, but her eyes were not. She'd had plenty of time to become accustomed to the sight of his bare legs and muscled chest with its inverted pyramid of blond hair. They'd spent many hours together dressed in shorts or bathing suits. Still, the thump of her heart at this moment must surely be loud enough for him to hear.

"You were right," he said. "The *pareo* is comfortable and cool." He added more to himself than to her, "And I've needed some cooling off lately."

They strolled between the vendors who lined either side of the pier: Their walk included ice-cream cones, soda pop, *pareos,* and shell jewelry.

Near the road stood a bright red carriage with yellow wheels. The rig was embellished with palm fronds and flowers, and the chestnut horse wore a crown of hibiscus and frangipani.

"Your carriage awaits," Cort announced with a grin.

"That's for us?" she asked in delight. "I didn't know Cinderella came in a Polynesian version."

"The glass slipper wouldn't have worked, because everybody goes barefoot here. And I suppose a papaya would be substituted for the pumpkin," Cort said. "But surely Polynesia has its Cinderella stories." His tone grew softer as he helped her into the carriage. "Don't you believe happily-ever-after can happen everywhere?"

Don't ask me to believe that. Don't ask me to start examining things and arriving at logical conclusions, she thought. "I believe happily-for-the-moment can happen anywhere."

"I'm not sure whether that's optimistic or cynical." He frowned.

He'd call it optimistic if he knew her recent past, she thought. But she said simply, "Did you tell the coachman that the ship sails before midnight?"

"So Cinderella's still afraid of missing the boat?"

She didn't know about Cinderella, but she did know Niera Pascotti was afraid of missing Cort Tucker long after the boat sailed, she admitted to herself.

It seemed natural for her to settle back into the curve of his arm as the carriage headed up the highway, passed by an infrequent car or motor scooter, and even by bicyclists. "This wouldn't make a good getaway vehicle," she commented before thinking. "Much too slow."

"Is there something you need to get away from?" he was quick to ask.

Her gaze wandered over his familiar features. "There's nothing I want to get away from at this moment."

"Glad to hear it." That usual light remark seemed somehow weighted down by a heavy underlayer she didn't understand.

They clip-clopped along the asphalt road bordered by multihued plants and blossoms, interspersed with tidy Tahitian houses. Alongside the mailboxes were long, slender boxes for the daily delivery of baguettes of

French bread. "One way to get dough in the mail," Cort remarked.

The carriage wound its way toward one of the coves along the Mooréa coast. An outrigger canoe manned by a strapping Polynesian rested at the water's edge.

"Can you stand to trade in your carriage before it turns into a papaya?" Cort asked, the pleasure in Niera's expression reflected in his.

She noticed a cooler and a box in the back of the outrigger. "Are we having a picnic?"

"Questions, questions, always questions," he replied in a tone that wasn't entirely teasing.

She had tried to make her questions subtle. But the fact that she was assailing him with an unusual number of queries apparently hadn't escaped him. As her emotional entanglement had grown, she'd worried that he might consider her stupid, always asking him to repeat some minor detail she'd heard a day or two before. She'd paid rapt attention to his every word, and now she recognized that would have been so in any case. Everything about Cort Tucker fascinated her, for entirely personal reasons.

The breeze whispered seductively in her ear as the outrigger moved across the lagoon. Aqua became turquoise, and turquoise became cerulean, as if pieces of sky had decided to go for a swim.

Earlier, she had wished that people could see through one another as easily as they could see through this crystalline water. Now she was glad that Cort couldn't see the intensity of her own feelings for him.

They stopped a few yards from a *motu*, one of the tiny coral atolls freckling the lagoon.

"The boatman can't bring the outrigger any closer to the atoll." Cort swung his legs over the side and stood in above-the-knees water.

Niera started to follow, but Cort scooped her into his arms and waded to the sugar-white shore. He let her down slowly, easily. Her body slid along his, and her bare thigh, escaping the slit in her *pareo,* brushed against his maleness beneath the thin cotton of his own garment.

"Wait right there," he breathed into her ear, just below the *tiare Tahiti* that proclaimed her availability.

He made two more trips between the outrigger and the shore, unloading the cooler and the other box.

"So it is a picnic," she said. "However did I guess? Mango sandwiches accompanied by ants wearing tiny flowers behind the appropriate antenna?"

"Not quite. And it can be either a picnic or a sit-down candlelight dinner. Your choice." He gestured beyond the grove of palm trees, and she saw the house for the first time.

The circular wooden building had a round pointed roof of palm thatch, like an upside-down cone. It appeared to float above the lagoon, perched on slender stilts. A narrow bridge of wood led from the edge of the sand to the house. It was the style Niera had come to think of as Polynesian posh.

She was surprised to hear the motor start up on the outrigger. Turning, she saw that the boatman was zipping toward Mooréa.

The humid air took on a sensual tangibility as she asked Cort, "When is he coming back?"

"Tomorrow." He watched uncertainly for her reaction. "About this same time."

"Oh," was all she could manage, simultaneously delighted and tremulous.

"I know it was presumptuous of me." His words rushed out. "Are you angry?"

Her glance encompassed most of the circumference of the palm-laden *motu.* "*Sortie de secours,*" she mumbled. "All this open space and no emergency exit." Her eyes returned to his.

"I was hoping you wouldn't want one. But there is a

flare gun in the house to summon help if you really want to leave." His expression begged her not to. "Or I can offer you an emergency lockup instead." He reached into the top of the box, then held out a key on a long chain. "You can sleep in the house, and I'll stay out here."

She realized she'd made this decision days ago and he'd sensed it. The opportunity had never been right until now. "You can keep the key," she murmured.

He bestowed a tender stroke along her bare shoulder and down her arm, ending with a squeeze of her hand. "Okay. I'd better get this stuff up to the house."

He hoisted the cooler.

"The box doesn't look too heavy for me to carry." She lifted it with little effort. "What's in here?"

"Food that didn't have to be chilled. A couple of extra *pareos* from my private stock. Toothbrushes, miscellaneous gear."

"You think of everything."

"I try to. But sometimes you seem to be off on some tangent I can't even guess at."

"Not tonight." She murmured that promise to him and to herself.

They walked through the palm grove. "This is the Tahitian wilderness," he warned her. "Try not to get bonked by a falling coconut."

"Do you happen to have a steel parasol among the miscellaneous items in this box?"

"Drat. I knew I forgot something." He grinned. "I did pack some mosquito repellent, though the owner assured me that we wouldn't need it. He sprays the entire island periodically, so the mosquitoes have all gone to live on other *motus.*"

Gingerly, they made their way across the rickety bridge and up the steps to the house. Cort unlocked the door to reveal one large circular room in which the furniture was placed so as to suggest a living area, a sleep space, and a kitchen area. There was an uncluttered space in the center of the house, and a curtained bathroom stood off to one side. The rattan sofa and chairs were cushioned in shades of lime and pineapple, and a pineapple-colored spread covered the waterbed, which was flanked by a rattan wardrobe and bureau. Windows offered sweeping views of Mooréa, the lagoon, and the ocean beyond.

"Very cozy," Niera remarked. "This looks like a private home."

"It is, for occasional weekends. The owner never rents it out, but he offered me the use of it. He's in the hospitality business, so anything that would promote Tahiti would benefit him. If I market *pareo* styles, Tahiti will be receiving an indirect plug."

Niera started toward the kitchen area, then stopped abruptly when she nearly stepped on a circle of thick glass set in the middle of the floor. Below her, the blue waters of the lagoon flashed with darts of golden sunlight.

"Do you suppose that's for us to watch the fish, or for the fish to watch us?" she quipped.

"Maybe we could teach some interesting lessons to schools of fish." He winked.

She glanced back at the floor window as she continued around to the kitchen area. "Tune in later for a *Flipper* rerun."

"I don't think we're quite that much like an old married couple yet." He casually concentrated on setting the cooler in place.

Yet. Niera tried to ignore that word. There was no sense in pinning her hopes on a lighthearted joke.

She set the box on a table and started to unpack the contents, but he caught her hand in his. "Let's not miss the sunset," he said. "Remember, I've always thought the colors of sunset were perfect for you."

Fingers laced together, they went outside and strolled

along the shore, watching as streaks of pink and peach swept across the horizon, surrounding them in brilliant hues.

Suddenly, a chill of sadness washed over her. Cort might not be here under false pretenses, but she was. "Sunset," she said. "The end of a bright day. A glorious ending, but an ending nonetheless."

"You're being pessimistic again. I was thinking of sunset as the herald of an even more fabulous night."

She tightened her grasp on his hand. "I like your way of thinking better."

"Remember that old standby pollster question?" he remarked as they sauntered on. "Who would you most like to be stranded on a desert island with? I've known the answer to that for days now."

He prompted her when she didn't respond, uncertainty edging into his tone. "Well?"

"My choice," she murmured, "is definitely somebody just like you."

"Just *like* me?" He tried to sound playful, but his seriousness was evident. "How about *me?*"

She laughed lightly, avoiding his direct gaze. "Want me to sign an affidavit? 'I hereby solemnly swear that I would like to be stranded on a desert island with Cort Tucker.'" The man I've known for the last week, she amended silently.

"I would like a signed affidavit to that effect, but my *pareo* has no pockets for a pen and paper."

They had ambled halfway around the *motu* when he stopped and pulled her into the crescent of his arm. The sun, a distant white-gold globe in a blaze of red-orange, cast a fiery patina on the water.

He took her other hand in his, caressing her palm with his thumb. The fire in the sky touched down and raced along her veins.

"This is our own private mystical isle, suspended in time," he said softly.

"Yes," she agreed on a sigh. But then she couldn't help withdrawing behind a barrier of patter. "Our own private *Brigadoon* in the *South Pacific,* a palm-strewn *Camelot* with a round house instead of a round table."

He lifted her hand, brushing his lips across the back. "Nothing but the best for *My Fair Lady.*"

"And since we have no *Cats,* I hope there are no rats on the island."

"We both have *High Hopes.*"

"Am I stranded with *The Music Man?*"

"I think we could make *A Little Night Music* together." His soft voice caressed her. "And the rainbows we'll spin won't be Finian's." He tucked her hand, still clasped in his, into the cradle of his neck and shoulder. "Now, is that enough of puns and general wittiness?"

"I d-don't know what you m-mean." She stammered out the fib.

"You're always backing away from me emotionally. Oh, you do it with panache. But it doesn't hurt any less." He released her hand, but she didn't move. "I thought maybe you were always joking because there were other people around. I hoped it would be different when we were alone."

She opened her mouth, wanting to explain, but no words came forth.

"Why do you always withdraw from me?" he asked, his eyes pleading. "And will you ever stop?"

She tilted her face upward toward his, in her own plea for that understanding. *"Sortie de secours,"* she said. "My attempts at humor are my emergency exit."

"But why are you always ready to run out?"

She slipped her hand away, allowing her fingers to trail longingly over his chest. Unable to meet his eyes, she stared into the red-orange horizon instead.

Swallowing hard, she forced herself to begin. "You said you wanted to be stranded on a desert island with me. But you don't really know me at all."

"You mean because we went through the introductions only a week ago? I feel as if we've known each other since the beginning of time." She could hear the new realization dawning in his tone. "Oh, you're afraid this is just a shipboard romance." He lowered his voice. "Well, for me, it's much more than that."

"For me, too," she hastened to assure him. "But you don't know who you're really sharing this *motu* with, because I haven't shared everything about myself with you."

"No, you haven't, as I well know. You've given me a verbal tour of Honolulu, and you've wittily discussed every imaginable subject—except yourself. You've talked a little about your childhood, but otherwise you shut me out. I assumed you didn't want to talk about yourself for some reason, and I didn't think I should push you before you were ready."

After a pause, she sighed. "We've kidded around about musical plays." She looked at him, directly, probingly. "Have you ever played a part?"

He appeared puzzled. "You mean like in college shows?"

"No. I mean in real life. Have you ever pretended to be someone else, taken on another identity, for any reason?"

He looked down, tracing patterns in the sand with his toe. It seemed as if an eternity passed before his eyes met hers and he answered, "I've never been anybody except plain old Cort Tucker."

She chose to believe him, because she *wanted* to believe him. Because it would have been intolerably agonizing not to believe him.

"Well," she said finally, taking her own turn at studying the sand, "I've played lots of roles. I've been doing it for years. In some ways, I've been acting a part this week. So I guess there are a few things I should tell you now."

His next words seemed to issue from a faraway void. "Is there another man?"

"No . . . at least not the way you mean." She looked back up at him, afraid to see his reaction, afraid not to see it. "When I told you I was in research, I was telling the truth, since *research* is another word for *investigation*. I'm an FBI agent."

He didn't look surprised. In fact, he managed a quick quip. "I don't require a warrant, if you want to conduct an extensive body search."

When her expression remained somber, he apologized. "Sorry. Now I'm the one who's being inappropriately frivolous. I can understand why you avoid telling people what you do for a living. I suppose you come up with some vague story about being in research, because people tend to be wary of law-enforcement officers."

Still she didn't continue, so he added with a grin, "Please don't tell me that you're a male agent disguised beneath that *pareo*."

She drew in a deep breath, then mustered enough courage to finish her story. "I'm under suspicion of criminal complicity by my own department. The case was one you'd find especially interesting, because of business. It involved counterfeit designer clothing."

"Are you sure you want to tell me about this?" he asked softly.

She nodded. He led her to a fallen palm tree. They sat down, and she ignored the roughness of the bark against her skin, which was protected only by the thin cotton *pareo*. Maintaining her resolve, she told him the whole story, omitting only the most confidential facts about the investigation. The sky darkened to hues of violet and blue while she explained as much as she could to him.

She finished with the painful summary, "So, you see,

the Bureau suspects that I acted in complicity with the criminals, maybe even plotted the death of my partner."

His only response was to put his arm around her shoulders and caress her upper arm comfortingly.

"Aren't you going to ask me if I'm guilty?" She forced the question out.

"I know you're not."

His words flooded her with relief and happiness.

He continued, "I wouldn't be here with you now if I thought you were capable of such a thing."

"Oh, Cort—"

His lips silenced her. His tongue slid across her lips, seeking and finding an opening, then probed inside, driving her into happy oblivion.

Their heat-laden kisses left them both gasping as darkness began to close around them.

It was Cort who managed to pull away. "We'd better get back to the house while we still have enough light to find our way. I don't want either of us to wind up with a broken neck from tripping over something in the dark."

The only thing she was tripping over was her feelings for him. And that was a long, delightful fall.

When they had crossed the islet, Cort brought their dinner from the house to the shoreline, and built a fire as much for illumination as for romantic atmosphere. "Too many cooks spoil the campfire," he remarked.

From the cooler, he produced two chilled glasses and a bottle of champagne.

"Darn," Niera said. "I was hoping for Dr Pepper. I've really missed that stuff in Tahiti." The selection of goods and merchandise was severely limited in French Polynesia, on shore as well as on the ship.

He bowed from the waist. "Sorry to have made a faux pas in offering mere French bubbly."

They dined on cold crab and chicken breasts, fresh mangoes, and a sort of Tahitian coleslaw made of shredded cabbage and carrots with papaya-seed dressing.

For the first time, Niera felt that their easy conversation was an open two-way communication, acknowledging that any prior barrier must have been the result of her own guilt at not being completely honest with him.

While they sipped the last of the champagne, she said, "This French drink gives me the urge to jump up and do a Tahitian hula."

"Please do," he responded with a lecherous lift of his eyebrows.

"If you really were the Music Man, you'd have a Tahitian combo, or at the very least a single drummer, here."

"Your wish is my command."

She watched in amused surprise as he levered himself up, went into the house, and returned a few minutes later with a cassette tape-player. He set it on the narrow strip of sand between the fire and the sea and switched on a tape of Tahitian music.

"I brought this in case we wanted to practice those hula techniques we learned yesterday. May I have this dance?"

He extended a hand to help her up, but she hesitated before accepting, engrossed in the play of the firelight over his tanned legs and chest, causing the sprinkling of light hair to gleam like latent embers. He leaned down, and the fire frolicked in highlights across his blond hair. For a moment, flames were reflected in miniature in his aquamarine eyes.

As Cort pulled her up beside him, she remembered that, for women, this dance involved only the hips in two elementary moves: from side to side and around in a circle. The original Tahitian *tamure* was simpler than its descendant, the Hawaiian hula. More basic. More direct.

As soon as she stood before him, he gently combed

his fingers through her hair, pausing over her left ear, above the *tiare Tahiti*.

"Available," he whispered.

"Only to you."

"Then you won't mind if I move this to the other side."

She shook her head slowly. A smile tilted his lips at the extra effort required to undo the bobby pins. Yet he made sure to fasten the blossom equally securely over her right ear. *Taken*.

Her heartbeat already outpaced the drums as she and Cort began to move to the taped music.

Her hips swayed from side to side, then around and around. Their Tahitian dancing on the ship had been but a tame imitation of this. She and Cort weren't touching yet, but their eyes joined them as one while they gyrated to the rhythm.

From side to side, around and around. Faster and faster. The tempo of the drumbeats increased.

Around and around. Faster and faster. The firelight licked across his chest.

Around and around. Faster and faster. Their undulating torsos were separated by inches.

Faster. Harder.

The pulse of the drums, the primitive need, penetrated to her core. Faster. Closer. Almost touching. Firelight glistened on the sheen of moisture coating their skin.

Faster. Closer. The fabric of their *pareos* brushed as their hips circled together. She was scarcely aware of water caressing her ankles as their movements took them to the edge of the sand. To the edge.

Faster. Closer. Soon. The drums pounded through her, vibrating along every nerve ending. The water mirrored the flame, which shimmered in the pathway of moonglow reflected on the surface.

Faster. Harder. Instinctively, their motions changed.

Not the censored twentieth-century *tamure,* but the rhythmic ritual that had throbbed along these islands in ancient times.

Not from side to side but back and forth, thrusting together.

Touching at last. Cort's hands roved over her, his breath coming in gasps like her own. His mouth ravaged hers, his tongue probing, then moving on. The fire was on his tongue, trailing a blaze over her lips, her cheek, her neck, and lower.

Nuzzling away the fold of her *pareo* over one soft mound of flesh, he captured its already blossoming tip between his lips. They sank to their knees at the edge of the lagoon.

"Cort, Cort ..." She breathed rather than spoke his name.

His hand entered the side slit in her *pareo,* caressing her thigh, gliding higher. His fingers slipped beyond her lacy panties, found her pulsing core, stroked through her warm liquid silk.

She melted against him—wanting him, needing him. Loving him.

He stroked back and forth, all around, at the hottest, most demanding point of her primitive need. She arched and writhed and quivered against him, clenching her fingers into his muscled shoulders, breathing his name until the moon shattered and sprinkled its glowdust on her.

The last pulsation had not yet faded away before the next thrummed along her veins.

"Oh, Niera, darling," Cort was whispering, untying the knot that held her *pareo* over her shoulder.

She glided her hand along the firm flesh of his waistline, then inside the fold of his *pareo* and downward. Her fingertips feathered the soft hair while he groaned in desire. She cradled his solid flesh in her hand.

He succeeded in untangling the knot, and her *pareo*

fell away. He spread the long rectangle of fabric on the sand, then lowered her back on it, all the time alternating kisses with the murmuring of her name. His hands were everywhere, caressing, tenderly squeezing. He slipped her panties off, his palms caressing the length of her legs.

"You're so beautiful," he gasped, his gaze sliding over her nakedness bathed in golden firelight and silvery moonlight.

Every cell of her being clamored for him. She tugged impatiently at his *pareo,* but it required Cort to reverse the complicated tucks. Before he flung it away, he unpinned a tiny packet that had been concealed in its folds.

"You really do think of everything," Niera whispered, pleased, continuing to caress him.

"I care about you too much to put you at any kind of risk," he murmured, before sealing his mouth to hers. Their tongues sampled and stroked each other in that final moment.

He lowered himself to her, pressing his cheek against hers. Into her right ear beneath the spicy fragrance of the *tiare Tahiti,* he whispered raggedly, "I didn't want to love you, but I couldn't stop myself, any more than I can stop myself right now."

A vague thought hovered in her mind. There was something she should ask him, something about why he didn't want to love her. But that thought was banished from her mind by her raging desire for him as she felt his solid masculinity against her taut thighs. His legs nudged her thighs apart. Her toes curled into the warm sand.

She arched to meet him in the sultry night. She shuddered with passion as she welcomed the length of his throbbing manhood into her softness.

There was only Cort, nothing but him, in her entire

universe. He was everything she wanted, present and future.

They moved together in harmonious rhythm, just as they had in the dance. Back and forth. Tender and gentle. Then faster and harder. Pounding together to the tempo of their hearts beating as one.

Then firelight and moonlight and blue lagoon and emerald jungle and burning sunlight all whirled across her senses as if in a kaleidoscope. Together, they cried out, "I love you," as they rocketed back across the ages and forward to the star-glazed future, knowing they were lovers for all time.

Chapter 7

NIERA AWOKE TO bright sunlight suffusing the room. An equally radiant smile lit her face as she recalled where she was, and with whom, and what they'd been doing all through the night.

Just when had they come inside the house? she wondered, then realized that it didn't matter. All that concerned her was the present, this brief, magical time with Cort. The waterbed undulated beneath her as she turned over to greet Cort with a kiss.

He wasn't there.

She blinked in surprise. But she realized he couldn't have gone far unless he'd hidden a submarine beneath the house.

Getting out of bed, she drew the top sheet around her like a maxi-*pareo*, and walked onto the balcony overhanging the lagoon, expecting a pleasant view.

The view was even better than she'd hoped.

Cort was out there, literally strolling on the turquoise lagoon.

"Hey," she yelled teasingly, "I waited a long time for Mr. Right, but I didn't expect him to walk on water."

"Anything for you," he shouted with a grin.

He strode toward her, balancing himself atop the coral reef that lay just beneath the surface of the water. Thick-soled canvas shoes protected his feet from cuts.

When he came in, he promptly embraced her with his arms and his smile. "There's a stack of *pareos* in the box, in case you want to change into something less comfortable. But I'd rather you didn't."

"*Pareos* really are handy. They can be used for everything from dresses to bathing suits."

"What I like best about them is that I can just unwrap you like a special Christmas present." He gave her an extra hug.

"You'll probably make a fortune if you market them in the States."

"I've already found my treasure." He rested his cheek against the top of her head. "Stay here with me, my treasure. The owner offered this place to me for three more days. When the boatman comes this afternoon, I'll tell him we're staying. He can bring us extra supplies and change our return-flight reservations."

Prolong the present. Postpone the future. She didn't hesitate before agreeing. "Okay."

They spent the day simply enjoying each other, the tropical setting an extra but unessential garnish to their passion. All day, she drifted in those aquamarine eyes that for her mirrored the depths of the ocean and the heights of the sky.

Finding a hammock, Niera stretched it between two palm trees at the appropriate height and taught Cort a new meaning for the word *swinger*. He expressed his approval in a series of moans and gasps beneath her as she bridged him, taking him into herself, twisting and pulsing above him until ecstasy launched them once again into a blazing orb.

When he was finally able to speak, he murmured in spent rapture, "I'm definitely growing a pair of palm trees in my bedroom as soon as I get home. You bring the hammock, okay?"

Her heart sang. It was the first time he'd alluded to any future together beyond the next three days.

After they returned to the house, he shaved while she sliced melon for a late lunch. He patted on some after shave, then walked over and embraced her from behind. The spicy-minty scent filled her nostrils.

"I like your after shave," she remarked.

"Thanks. You've just given me a testimonial as well as a compliment. It's an original scent that was created for Dressed for Excess. We're thinking of marketing it to women as a gift for their men."

Niera froze in Cort's arms. If the fragrance was one-of-a-kind, how could she remember it from Honolulu?

She didn't remember it, of course. That was the answer. She'd smelled something similar while she was in the hospital.

Still, a new doubt took seed in her mind.

She accompanied Cort when he told the English-speaking boatman of their change in plans.

When Cort was finished, Niera gave the boatman a note for Megan, and made another special request of him. "Please have my return ticket changed in destination as well as day. It's currently for Honolulu, but I'll be going to Los Angeles instead."

Cort looked at her in surprise.

"I have to report in at the FBI office in Los Angeles before I return to Honolulu," she said, feeling a terrible twinge at lying to him. Actually, she had decided her final destination would be Denver. She wished she could stifle this last smidgen of doubt about Cort's business, but it burned within her like a stubborn ember from last night's fires, and she knew the only sure way to extinguish it was to check for herself.

When the boatman returned with the extra supplies, Niera remarked, "I hope it isn't inconvenient for you or your boss that we stay longer."

He grinned. "Time means little in Tahiti. The natives have a saying: 'Yesterday was yesterday, today is really today, tomorrow is another day.'"

He had no idea how appropriate that was for her, Niera mused. But she covered her turbulent emotions with a quip to Cort. "How about that? Scarlet O'Hara must have passed through Tahiti on her way to Tara."

Their next days were idyllic. Niera managed to forget that they'd ever have to leave, and that she'd be surreptitiously going to Denver when they eventually did leave.

On their fourth and last day, she was rummaging in her purse for lipstick when she discovered a scrunched-up old box of licorice candy. Reluctantly, she pulled it out. This was the same fawn-colored handbag that she'd been carrying before she left Honolulu; she'd stuck the box of candy in there, she recalled, when she and Royce had gone to a special showing of the 1956 musical movie *Carousel*.

She knew for certain now that Cort didn't smoke, or had given it up, since she'd been with him constantly for four days.

But had he been avoiding licorice by choice or by plan? Or was that particular candy unavailable in Tahiti, like so many other things people took for granted in the United States?

He sauntered in from the balcony as she was still staring at the small box in her hand. "What have you got there?" he asked cheerfully, just making conversation.

"Licorice," she replied. "I forgot it was in my purse. Want some?"

"Yuck. I hate licorice."

He seemed both puzzled and delighted to learn that hating licorice was worth a passionate kiss from her.

At lunchtime, while she was searching for the salt, Niera came across a container and cleaner for contact lenses.

She looked back at Cort, who was setting the table. She wasn't about to waste time on a subtle interrogation. "I didn't know you wore contact lenses," she said sharply.

"That's because mine are the kind that can be left in for a couple of weeks," he answered easily. "All the better to see you with. And since I'm nearsighted, the nearer you are the better." He passed by her, brushing a kiss across her cheek. "Or maybe my condition could be more accurately diagnosed as *Niera*-sighted."

When she didn't comment, he prompted, "Love me anyway?"

Utter somberness etched her features as she said, "I do love you."

Nonetheless, she couldn't resist leaving the licorice where Cort could find it. She counted the pieces, so she could know later whether any were missing. With all her heart, she hoped none would be.

They spent the rest of the afternoon snorkeling and sunbathing.

Their final sunset was daubing the sky beyond a puffy echelon of clouds when Niera stepped out of the shower, drying her hair. She stopped short when her gaze fell on the spot where she'd left the candy box. She needn't have bothered counting the pieces, since the entire package was gone.

She wrapped herself in a fresh *pareo*, suddenly self-conscious at the thought of being nude in Cort's presence.

She found him on the balcony, the yellow and red candy box crushed in his hand.

"Hi," he said with a smile, slipping his arm around

her waist. Several butterfly fish swarmed below them. "These silly fish adore stale licorice."

Seeing her stunned expression, he added, "You don't mind my feeding it to them? It was so old, I didn't figure you'd want it."

"It's okay," she muttered, wondering how many of those pieces had actually wound up in fishy tummies. "I hope they don't get cavities."

"Maybe it will serve them well. The next big fish that comes along and starts to eat one of these fellows may spit him back out, if it hates licorice as much as I do."

Right, she reminded herself. Big fish swallow up little fish. Time to go back to the real world—physically, mentally, and emotionally. It was a purely intellectual decision, she told herself, to tilt her head up for a kiss. Would there be a residual taste of licorice in that moist, warm mouth that had given her so much pleasure in so many ways?

Instead, he planted a quick kiss on her forehead and pulled away teasingly. "Last one in is a rotten barracuda," he tossed back, jumping off the edge of the balcony into the water.

That night was the blackest black Niera had ever experienced. If the moon and stars were still up there in the sky, clouds were obscuring them.

In that total darkness, she couldn't help once again losing herself completely to her lover, a man she couldn't see tonight but who tenderly and exquisitely brought her again and again to the brink of ecstasy, then launched them over the edge together. They created their own universe, their own moon and stars.

The glow of their private moon and stars waned, and Niera lay almost asleep in his arms, musing that this night was as black as licorice.

Apparently sharing a similar thought but in a more romantic mode, he murmured, "Tonight is like a black pearl."

A black pearl. Round and perfect, it nestled deep in the center of a fragrant, creamy cradle formed by the half-open petals of a *tiare Tahiti*.

It was their last day in Paradise. They had been on their way to the airport on the island of Tahiti when Cort had asked their cab driver to stop at a quiet cove. Then he had taken her hand in his to walk one final time to the edge of the sea.

"Oh, Cort," Niera sighed, running a fingertip over the soft petals enclosing his latest gift.

She looked up into his face, the face she knew she loved, framed by the turquoise lagoon shimmering in the sun. He was watching her eagerly, expectantly, with a touch of little-boy uncertainty that tugged at her heart.

"The jewel is free," he said softly, "not trapped in any permanent setting. It can become anything you want." His gaze caressed her. "I'm hoping you'll be willing to sacrifice a little of that freedom so the pearl can become the center of a wedding ring."

"Cort." Niera breathed his name without conscious thought. "I love you, but it's not that simple."

"We've been simply enjoying each other for days." He grasped her hand, tightening his fingers in a grip that was almost painful and that seemed to reflect the desperation in his tone. "We don't have to go back. We can find our own *motu,* or we could buy a yacht and sail around the world. Anything you want. Just stay with me now."

"Oh, darling." She glanced down at the pearl and the blossom. "If only everything were that easy, if only everything were distinctly black or white, like this."

"Nothing is ever clear-cut," he said. He turned her

hand, then clasped her other hand in his, spilling the gem into her open palm. "Not even this." He gently rocked her hand, causing the pearl to roll back and forth. "See? Even this pearl isn't entirely black. It's those subtle shadings that give it character, make it precious. Look at the luster of blue and green in the light."

He was right. The black pearl was luminescent with other hues. Shadows and shadings.

Layer upon layer of attractive camouflage, disguising the true interior.

She closed her eyes for a moment, shutting out the sight of the pearl, of him. It would be wonderful if only she could remain suspended in time with the man she loved. If only. . .

Swallowing hard, she opened her eyes to see him still watching her, his own eyes a silent, almost despairing plea.

"Maybe someday." Oh, if only that could come true! "Maybe soon," she whispered. "It's a wonderful dream."

"Dreams can be future realities. And our future can start right now."

"No, no, it can't," she declared, forcing herself to pull away from him. "You have a business to run, and I have a case to solve."

"The only thing I can't stand to be finished with is you. If you loved me a fraction as much as I love you, you'd want to prolong our time together. You'd want it to last forever."

She did want to prolong it, desperately, recklessly. Could happiness be that simple, that easy?

Her body swayed toward him, as the decision was swaying her mind. But she couldn't touch him, couldn't let him touch her, for fear of forfeiting all control and rationality.

"If we're meant to be together, our love will flourish

wherever we are, even if we're separated in place and time for a while," she said finally.

"I hope you're right," he murmured, not meeting her eyes.

"If I'm not, then it wasn't a love worth trying to hold on to, no matter how we feel at this moment."

She held out her open palm to him, returning the expensive jewel. Cradling that hand in his, he tenderly closed her fingers over the pearl. "You keep it. It's yours for whatever use you want to make of it. When you're ready to make a final decision, I'll be waiting."

They caught the eight-hour flight to Los Angeles, where Cort expected her to remain while he caught a connecting flight to Denver. He was napping, but her mind was galloping too fast for her to doze off.

The plane dipped into an air pocket, awakening Cort abruptly. Blinking, he exclaimed, "One of my contact lenses popped out." He bent over and began feeling around on the floor.

Niera froze for an instant before she could bring herself to lean forward and join him in the search. She could scarcely breathe, waiting for the moment when he'd look in her direction, or find the lens.

"Here it is," he proclaimed triumphantly.

Niera soared far higher than an airplane could reach when she saw that the lens balanced on his fingertip was untinted, and that he was looking straight at her with those gorgeous, all-his-own aquamarine eyes.

"Oh, Cort," Niera grabbed him and planted a kiss on his cheek.

He reacted with surprised enthusiasm. "I would have lost a lens sooner if I'd known the effect it would have on you." He kissed her right back, bigger and better and square on the lips.

* * *

"Come to Denver as soon as your business here is finished," Cort was urging her as they strode down the concourse at Los Angeles International Airport. The plane had circled over the Pacific for forty minutes, waiting for the fog to clear enough to land. "Or better yet, I'll postpone my flight and stay with you; then we'll fly to Denver together."

Thrills ran amok along her veins at the realization that Cort was inviting her to Denver. That must mean his story was true.

Still, now that she was so close to being certain of him, she really ought to carry out that final investigation.

They exchanged addresses and telephone numbers, and she saw him off for Denver as if he were a soldier going to war.

But it was she who had a private war to finish, she reminded herself, as she boarded a different plane for Denver three hours later. She hoped that Cort Tucker's true identity had nothing to do with that war.

Chapter   8

SUNRISE WAS THE same shade of pink halfway around the world, even in Denver, where it was winter instead of eternal summer, Niera mused as she parked her rented Ciera around the corner from the cul-de-sac in the exclusive suburb of Greenwood Village. A large stone house stood at the apex of the curve, at the address Cort had given her.

She snuggled deeper into the nondescript gray down coat she'd bought last night. She was glad that her new brunette wig provided some protection for her ears. The fact that she couldn't leave the engine running for fear of attracting attention to the car, and therefore couldn't leave the heater on, reminded her why she preferred stakeouts in Hawaii.

She had slept restlessly, tossing all night, in her room at a nearby Hilton Inn. It had seemed strange, and very wrong, for her to be in that bed alone when Cort was less than a mile away.

Despite her near-sleepless night, the icy temperature kept her from dozing off in the hours between sunrise until eight A.M., when the door of Cort's house finally opened.

Only it wasn't Cort who emerged.

Niera stiffened, her hands clenching the steering wheel as if it were a life preserver.

Coming out of Cort's house was a beautiful slim woman with flaxen hair.

Maybe she was watching the wrong house? The streets curved around so much . . .

A black and white bundle of energy scampered out of the house and danced around the woman's feet.

Cort's Sheltie. Her heart plummeted as she identified this furry accomplice.

The woman turned back toward the house and held open her arms.

Her arms were instantly filled by Cort! He wore a burgundy bathrobe tied loosely around his waist.

Niera could scarcely bring herself to watch as they hugged each other, finally parting with an exchange of kisses on the cheek.

Innocent until proven guilty, Niera tried to remind herself.

As the woman drove away in a baby-blue Jaguar, Niera ducked down, noting the license number. The pencil's lead snapped under pressure before she'd written down the last numeral.

Never had she watched a subject under surveillance with such longing, with such a heated hunger spiraling within her, as when she watched Cort go back inside the house, then drive away a half-hour later in a red Mercedes.

She knew that Dressed for Excess had its headquarters in Greenwood Office Park and a branch office at the Denver Merchandise Mart on the opposite side of town.

She followed at a safe distance only long enough to

see Cort turn into the maze of streets leading to Greenwood Office Park. She wanted to complete her other
checking before going there.

Stopping at the county clerk's office, she dutifully
verified first that the red Mercedes was registered to
Cort Tucker. Then she checked the license number of
the blue Jaguar.

"That's wonderful!" She couldn't help the words
escaping her lips as relief washed over her.

"Sure you're not in the wrong office?" the clerk
asked with a grin. "We usually see that kind of happiness only in the marriage-license line."

Niera couldn't stop beaming. The Jaguar was registered to Janette Tucker, Cort's sister. She'd been taking
care of his dog, Niera recalled.

It didn't take long to review other public documents,
including his house deed. The secretary of state's office
confirmed that Cort Tucker had been president of
Dressed for Excess, Inc., since the corporation was ini-
tially registered five years ago.

Still, the FBI could have planted the false documen-
tation if the Bureau was using Cort for some reason.
There was even a possibility that Dressed for Excess
could be an elaborate sting operation set up to gather
evidence against persons and organizations engaged in
counterfeiting designer clothing.

Niera continued her investigation, questioning Cort's
relatives and neighbors, and employees at both of the
offices. She learned that Dressed for Excess had
boomed to rapid success, was a respected company, and
had been in business about five years.

She practically skipped like an elated child into the
Dressed for Excess headquarters. Her heart and her out-
look were loftier than the towering violet peaks of the
Rocky Mountains, visible on the western horizon. She
had shed her down coat, which was much too heavy
now that the temperature had risen to sixty-degrees.

There was no receptionist at the desk in the outer office of Dressed for Excess. Niera paced impatiently for a while, then decided to go into the inner office unannounced.

Just then the door was opened from the other side by a stunning, willowy model with titian hair, wearing a *pareo* that Niera recognized as one of the stock Cort had purchased on Bora Bora.

"Hi," the woman greeted cheerfully. "Ida must have stepped away. Anything I can do for you?"

"I'm looking for Cort Tucker."

"Well, let's see," the woman said with an appraising, friendly grin, "you're too short to be a model, so it must be personal." She feigned a long sigh. "The one boss some of us wouldn't mind a little personal attention from refuses to mix business with pleasure."

Niera smiled back giddily. One more piece of great news.

"Whoops. Hi, boss," the woman said over Niera's shoulder.

Niera turned and started eagerly toward Cort, noting only peripherally that he looked great in a conservative brown tweed business suit worn with a burnt orange shirt.

He didn't look happy to see her. After greeting the model, he took Niera's arm and ushered her into the hallway. She didn't pull away, too glad to feel his touch once again. She searched his face for a sign that he was pleased to see her, but his features seemed carved of granite.

"We can talk privately without interruptions at my house," he said in frozen tones. "I'm sure you know the way."

He stalked off, leaving her to scurry after him. "Cort!" she called out.

"Not here," he tossed over his shoulder.

He idled his red Mercedes at the parking lot exit only

long enough to see her start her car engine, then peeled onto the street. She caught up with him at a red light.

They inched across town in the rush hour traffic on I-25. Niera took advantage of a halt in the jammed traffic to shrug into her coat again, for as soon as the sun dipped behind the mountains, the bitter chill returned.

And her cheerful, smiling Cort—the man who might have been her eternal summer—had become an arctic glacier.

At last, he turned into his driveway. She pulled in behind him, blocking his retreat. He couldn't escape via either Mercedes or scuba tanks this time. But he appeared ready to confront rather than run.

He was unlocking the front door as she reached his side. The little black and white Sheltie jumped and wriggled in exultant greeting as they entered the house.

"Niera Pascotti, meet Rambunctious Tucker, a.k.a. Ramby." Cort's words were clipped as he knelt to pet the dog. "He's probably the only one you haven't interrogated today."

"Cort, I'm sorry, but—"

"Well, go ahead," he interrupted. "Ask Ramby anything you want. After all, he actually lives with me, unlike the others you've questioned. Of course, his answers may be biased. He tends to be loving, faithful, trusting—qualities I'm sure you don't acquire while working for the FBI."

Sighing, waiting for his anger to spend itself, she knelt to pat the dog, who was far more welcoming than his master.

"Did you think I was too stupid to figure it out?" he grumbled. "All the calls I've had—neighbors, colleagues, relatives—reporting that a petite brunette was questioning them about me. Did you think I couldn't guess who the woman was, despite the wig?"

Turning his back on her, he strode into an enormous living room. She followed him. A fireplace stood in the center of a stone wall. Otherwise, she registered an innovative color scheme of pastels mingled with earth tones and an intriguing combination of textures that included velvet, leather, and silk. Cort evidently appreciated contrasts.

"What did you plan to do next?" he demanded. "I suppose you went to my office to pump my employees for information about my sexual liaisons."

"I went there to see you," she snapped, deciding that the well of his rage wasn't going to run dry. "I was going to tell you how I'd spent my day, and why."

"I know why. You couldn't allow yourself to love me without investigating me to see whether I was worthy of you."

"Don't do that. Please don't," she whispered, the words catching in her throat.

Concern for her flashed on his face, then was banished. But his voice sounded softer. "Don't do what?"

"Don't diminish what was between us on the *motu,* and before. You know how completely, how totally, I loved you then. I still do." She couldn't prevent a layer of tears from glazing her eyes, but she willed them not to fall.

His eyes merged into hers for a long moment; then he glanced away. "Okay." His quiet tone signaled an end to his tirade. "What explanation did you intend to offer for your conduct today?"

"Cort, I had to make certain that you were the man you claimed to be. You know I'm involved in an unsolved case, one in which I'm a suspect. A case that involves faked designer clothing."

"So you thought I might be a crook?" Astonishment and pain blended in his question.

"Of course not. The criminals know I'm not one of them. They'd have no reason to watch me."

"Then what?"

"I thought you might be an FBI agent, too, assigned

to watch me. For a while, I even thought you might be . . ." Her last words trailed off.

"Might be what?"

"Nothing." She made a dismissive gesture. "It was foolish." She couldn't bring herself to reveal that she'd thought he might be another man entirely.

"Tell me." It was a murmur rather than a command.

She told only a little of the truth. "I saw a man who looked like you a couple of times at the hospital in Honolulu."

He turned away from her and placed a log in the fireplace. She hoped that symbolized a rekindling of his warm feelings toward her, but he continued to avoid her eyes.

He stoked and poked until flames embraced the log in a fiery clasp.

Then he stood, his gaze drowning her in aquamarine depths. "So am I all checked out to your satisfaction?"

A smile curled around her mouth. "Absolutely."

His lips quirked in a responding grin. "You kind of remind me of a gorgeous blonde I love."

You kind of remind me of a dark-haired man I used to know. The thought skidded across her mind, but she said nothing aloud, preferring to focus solely on the man before her. Her smile widened.

"All day long," he said, "I kept picturing you at my front door, in my office. Then, when you did appear, I acted like a crazy man in different ways than I'd expected to. I guess I didn't like my associates and friends being questioned about me."

"That's a normal reaction."

"Come on over here." He opened his arms to her. "And let's get rid of that cumbersome wig."

She slipped off her coat and walked into his arms. He hugged her close for a moment; then his fingers sought out and dispatched the bobby pins holding her wig in place. He tossed it aside.

He laced his fingers into the blond strands, slowly combing through her hair, fluffing it around her up-turned face.

"I think this blonde's about to have more fun," she murmured.

"So's this one."

As he bent his head to kiss her, they were interrupted by a low growl. Ramby was playing with his new toy—her wig—holding it between his teeth and shaking it so quickly it was almost a blur.

"One non-blond dog is having fun, too," Cort commented with a laugh.

"He gyrates even faster than those Tahitian dancers."

"Speaking of Tahiti"—he pulled her against him—"and gyrations..."

He kissed her, and their mouths continued to pleasure each other while zippers whispered open and clothes pooled around their ankles. His lips and tongue bathed the length of her body with liquid heat as they sank together to the plush carpet in front of the fireplace.

Once again, firelight danced over them in shadows and flickers, but it was Cort, always and only Cort, who set her body ablaze. They loved each other past the highest pinnacles of ecstasy, yet always wanted more, while the flames swirled and crackled and sizzled.

Much later, she sat enveloped in Cort's far-too-large but toasty burgundy robe. Laughter bubbled out of her like a fountain when she saw him returning from the kitchen with two crystal goblets. He wore only a patch-work apron tied around his waist. "Now, that looks far more ridiculous than a *pareo*," she said with a giggle.

"That wasn't a nice remark to make." He feigned distress. "Especially after I brought your favorite drink." He eased down beside her. "Fortunately, I'm secure in my masculinity. Especially with you around." He kissed her cheek. "And that robe you're wearing isn't going to set any fashion trends."

"I warned you before that I'm not an up-to-the-minute trendy dresser."

"As long as you're a timely undresser." He wiggled his eyebrows.

She took a sip of the dark, fizzy beverage he handed her. "Dr Pepper!"

"As I told you, I had hopes that you'd turn up here. I wrote it on my housekeeper's shopping list this morning."

They sat cozily, Niera fitting happily into the niche of his arm. Her glance fell on the nearby bookcase.

"Is that your college yearbook?" she asked.

"Oops," he answered with a laugh.

"I take it that means yes. Come on," she tickled him playfully, "let me see."

"I guess you might as well view some of my past, since we're going to be each other's future." He retrieved his college annuals and a family album containing photographs of Cort and his sisters at all ages, along with his parents. She was pleased that he seemed to value these mementos as well as recent pictures of his sisters, and the families of those who were married. Photos of Ramby made up a good share of the contents of the album, too.

"Sure you're not bored?" he asked a couple of times.

"Never with you, never with anything about you."

They fixed a very late dinner of cheese omelets and bacon, then wandered toward Cort's bedroom with their arms around each other's waists.

"You'd better set the alarm clock for four A.M.," she remarked. "I have to go back to the Hilton, pack, check out, and get to the airport in time for the first flight to Honolulu."

She felt his body stiffen.

"What do you mean? You're not leaving again? Not right away?"

"Unless the case was solved while we were in Tahiti,

I still have criminals to catch. Which, by the way, will clear me of suspicion so I can be sure of having a future to share with you."

"Stay here. Give us a chance," he pleaded.

"That would be irrelevant if I went to prison because some other agent didn't do as good a job of solving this as I could," she pointed out. The oversize robe suddenly felt heavy on her shoulders, weighing her down like a mantle of the past from which she needed to free herself.

Cort was usually so intelligent, so reasonable. She couldn't understand why he became totally irrational whenever they had this discussion. It was a replay from less than two days ago, when they were halfway around the world. He wanted them to stay together now, no matter what.

The atmosphere between them became heated in a new, different, and very unwelcome way. The volume of their voices increased.

"Just incidentally," she pointed out dryly, "by finding these crooks, I'll not only be clearing myself; I'll also be avenging the murder of my partner. I don't consider that a small matter."

Cort reacted as if she had physically hit him. She couldn't begin to identify every one of the varied emotions battling for control of his features. After a long pause, he said in a deadly quiet tone, "That's right. It's no small matter. But I don't want *you* to wind up the same way."

"Is that what's bothering you?" She launched herself toward him, twining her arms around his neck. "Darling, I'll be all right. I promise."

Cort's arms remained at his sides, and after several seconds, Niera got the message and pulled away from him, her eyes mirroring a puzzled entreaty.

"Surely you're not the only reliable agent in the FBI? They're relentless in finding murderers of other law-enforcement officers and in defending their own against unjustified suspicion."

She didn't answer immediately.

"If you love me," he said softly but firmly, "you'll forget the past and stay with me."

"I do love you. I can't believe that you don't understand why I can't stay right now. We'll be together again."

"If you insist on going back to Honolulu, it could all be over for us."

"If it could be over that fast, that easily, then it isn't worth having."

She pivoted away from him and began gathering up her clothes. He made no further attempt to stop her as she dressed in the bathroom. Her heart plummeted further when she saw he hadn't waited in the living room to tell her good-bye. She let herself out through the front door.

She gasped, surprised to encounter Cort standing on the front step. His bare chest peeked from his half-buttoned winter coat, but he had taken the time to pull on a pair of trousers. His hands were stuffed in his coat pockets.

His gaze wandered over her. Then he looked away, saying merely, "Take care of yourself."

"You, too," she murmured, rushing past him.

She blinked away the tears blurring the headlights of oncoming cars as she drove the short distance to the Hilton Inn. Somehow, she kept expecting to see Cort— at the hotel, at the airport the next morning. But he was never there.

Her connecting flight was delayed for three hours, since the first plane had been unable to land on schedule at Los Angeles because of dense winter fog. When her flight finally landed in Honolulu, she dragged herself off the plane, a walking combination of jet lag and sheer fatigue.

Suddenly, she was grasped from behind, someone's hands locking over her eyes in a fleshy blindfold.

"Guess who?" a man's voice asked.

That deep voice. Honolulu. The only possible name quavered out of her throat. "Royce!"

Chapter 9

"ROYCE..."

As the man repeated, with an undertone of despair, the name she'd spoken, Niera caught a whiff of spicy-minty fragrance.

His hands slipped away from her face, brushing over her shoulders. She turned in disbelief. "Cort!"

"I guess you were expecting somebody else," Cort muttered.

"How did you get here?" Surprised pleasure beamed on her face, but he didn't return her smile.

"Same as most people," he said wryly.

"You were on my flight and you didn't sit with me?"

"I took a later flight. It just got here sooner because yours was delayed in Los Angeles. Five minutes after you left Denver, I started to miss you as if you'd been gone for five years. I realized I was being a jerk. I should be helping you solve this case, not trying to hold you back."

147

"Oh, darling—"

This time his arms welcomed her, and they clung to each other for several minutes.

He brushed a kiss across her lips.

She yawned.

"Was it only last night you said you'd never be bored with me?" His chuckle vibrated through her.

"I'm sorry. I'm just so tired."

"Me, too. Maybe we ought to literally sleep together tonight."

"Oh, darn."

"Is that a rejecting darn, meaning you don't want to sleep with me? Or a complimentary darn, meaning you don't want to *just* sleep with me?"

"It's a darn-my-apartment darn. It hasn't been cleaned in months." Her thoughts wrenched as she remembered how thoroughly she had cleaned it on her last day in Honolulu so that everything would be perfect for her candlelight dinner with Royce. The table would still be set for a romantic dinner for two, the red candle still twisting in its silver holder.

"Let's stay at a hotel tonight." A strange sense of foreboding wove through his next words. "We don't have to face the past quite yet."

She took her mind on a quick stroll through her mental Yellow Pages. Practically every hotel in Honolulu was tangled in her memory with some case. Surveillance at one. Security for visiting dignitaries at another. An undercover assignment at still another.

And not the kind of undercover projects she was interested in with Cort.

At last, the perfect place occurred to her, where they could hold yesterday at bay for a few hours longer. "There's a new hotel, the Waikiki Parc. It's about the only one I've never been in."

His lifted eyebrows teased her.

"I mean on a case. You know."

"I'm glad you want someplace special just for you and me."

"It's kind of far from here, though, at the other end of Waikiki."

"I can make it if you can." He grinned at her.

They took a cab, as they were both too tired to drive a rented car. Cradled in Cort's arms, Niera closed her eyes to the sights of her yesterdays whizzing by, and dozed until the cab stopped.

Hazily, she came awake. "Here the past and the present come together," she said drowsily. "The old and the new."

She pointed, explaining to Cort, "Over there is the Halekulani, one of the three oldest hotels in Honolulu, built around 1917. A new building was constructed recently around the original main building and courtyard." The new layered over the old on a grand scale.

"And here," she gestured at the high-rise beside them, "is the newest hotel of all, the Waikiki Parc."

"A French name in Honolulu?"

"This is a town with something for everyone," she said, as they climbed out of the cab. "Hawaii is the favorite foreign vacation spot of the Japanese, and they love European touches. Japanese tourists like to shop for European merchandise with designer labels at the boutiques along Waikiki."

"Isn't that stuff overpriced?"

"Not when you figure that a Gucci bag that sells for one hundred fifty dollars here would cost twice as much in Tokyo."

Damn, Niera thought, as soon as the words were out of her mouth. Why did she keep twisting the knife in the wounds of her own memories? Ever since her plane had landed here, her past had been pummeling its way into her present.

"I suppose that's why this is a prime market for

bogus designer merchandise," Cort remarked, as they entered the hotel lobby.

"Right." She clipped off the word, and mercifully Cort didn't pursue that line of conversation.

He requested a room on the top floor. As they rode up in the elevator, Niera supposed that the twenty-second story was as far as she could get from her memories in Honolulu.

Awakening the next morning, she yawned and stretched. An eager joy radiated through her as she realized she couldn't stretch far without encountering Cort, who was curled around her.

He was already awake, watching her, the corners of his lips tilted upward in a slight but somehow sad smile. "I was waiting for you to open your eyes," he said. "That wonderful gray like the first light of dawn. My very own dawn."

Wrapping her in his arms, he brushed a kiss above each eye, then let his lips trail across her cheek. "Make love to me one more time," he breathed a plea into the shell of her ear.

Caught up in the slide of his flesh against hers, his firm body against her softness, their hearts beating as one, she murmured, "Always, darling. One more time is just a start."

His lovemaking was as exciting as always, yet it was mingled with the special tenderness of his desperate desire to claim her, to make her his forever. Over and over she shuddered against him as the supreme ecstasy shattered her senses, but he didn't yet choose that final release for himself. He remained inside her, intimately stroking or intimately still, while she writhed and gasped and quivered beneath him.

"Oh, Cort, Cort," she breathed, over and over. "I didn't know it could be like this."

And he prolonged the present, blocking everything

ut himself from her thoughts, while the sun rose higher over the horizon, until at last they rocketed toward it together in their own fiery, galactic swirl.

Later, they showered together, not wanting to be apart. Then Niera dressed while he shaved. She was standing on the balcony when he embraced her from behind, and she rested the back of her head on his chest.

"It's the same ocean," Cort murmured, as they watched waves scalloped in lacy foam kiss the pale sand, then recede, leaving a little of themselves behind. "Those could be the very same waves we saw in Tahiti —they've traveled all this distance to catch up with us."

The sooner she could settle everything, the better. With false cheerfulness, she asked, "Ready for breakfast?"

"I think lunch is more appropriate. It's almost check-out time." His arms tightened around her almost painfully for a moment. "Then we'll go to your apartment. We have some things to talk about."

She hoped he hadn't come here just to try to talk her into leaving right away with him. She was glad to postpone a replay of their usual discussion on that subject until after lunch.

They checked out, leaving their bags at the desk, then went to one of the hotel restaurants.

As they took first nibbles of their appetizers, Niera's small bite seemed to stick in her throat, and her hand froze in midair.

"What's wrong?" Cort asked.

She couldn't take her eyes off the man crossing the room.

Hal Symons, her boss.

He began speaking as he neared their table, approaching from behind Cort. "Niera. I didn't know you were back."

"I arrived late last night. I was planning to call you today."

Hal was continuing around the table, watching Niera. "You're looking much better than when I last saw you."

"I'm fine. And ready to resume my duties." She could read nothing in the bland expression of the veteran agent.

Hal's glance flicked away from her, in Cort's directions, and pure shock flashed on his features. "Cort Tucker! I thought you went back to Denver weeks ago!"

A seering agony spiraled through Niera, the tortured pain reflecting in her eyes as she stared at Cort. But she willed herself not to lose all control in front of Hal.

Silence set the scene in stone.

Niera mustered a smidgen of resolve, calling on anger to vanquish the pain, at least for this moment. "I should have known," she said coolly. "There's a saying in the counterfeit-merchandise game: If a bargain looks too good to be true, it probably isn't."

She turned her icy gaze on Hal. "So you're the proud owner of this genuine phony."

"No—" Hal started.

"He may be on loan from another FBI office," she said, "but he's still yours to play with, isn't he?"

"No—" Hal got out only that same word of protest before Niera interrupted him again.

"By the way, that's some elaborate sting operation the FBI has set up in Denver."

A frown added to the furrows in Hal's brow. "I don't know what you're talking about, Niera."

"Him." She pointed a derisive thumb at Cort.

"You don't know who he is?"

"Not fully, it seems."

Cort spoke at last. "I'm Royce Taggart's brother."

Hal insisted on talking to each of them separately. The hotel offered him the use of a small unoccupied office for that purpose. Before being individually interviewed by Hal, Niera and Cort made a pact to meet later on the beach near the hotel.

Niera lingered near the water, as agreed, waiting for Cort, letting rage and curiosity disguise her pain just a little longer.

At last she sensed rather than saw him beside her. "Such a fine line between illusion and delusion. It's like trying to hold on to one of those waves that makes a quick, smashing impact, then slides away." Niera whispered the words, not looking at Cort.

"Hit-and-run is for waves, not for people." He spoke in a murmur, but his deep tones reverberated through her. "I don't want to go away, like the waves. Please don't make me."

Niera shut her eyes against the azure sea and the relentless sun. If only she could shut out the last two weeks so easily.

Cort placed his hand gently on her arm, but she shrugged it off.

"I never lied to you, you know," he said.

"Oh, sure you didn't." At last she shifted her gaze to him, her eyes flinging silver daggers.

"I admit to one, and only one, little fib right after we met, when I said I'd never been to Hawaii. But after that, everything I told you was the absolute truth."

"That's right. You told the absolute truth in your fashion, omitting only a few minor facts."

"I suppose you've pieced together the details by now, from your conversation with Hal."

"Why don't you run it by me, in case stupid little ole me has missed some other 'minor' points," she demanded sardonically.

Her own pain seemed mirrored in his aquamarine eyes, so she refused to look at him, staring out over the ocean while he talked over her shoulder.

He drew a long breath, sighed, drew another, then began. "Royce Taggart was my half brother, by my father's first marriage. I never knew Royce existed until I went through some papers of my father's after he died. His first wife had moved away and they hadn't kept in touch." His voice caught. "I'm sorry to say that my father, a man I had always admired, apparently made no effort to care for his firstborn son. I don't understand that about him. I'm sure that he loved my mother's three daughters by her first husband as much as he loved my sister and me."

"It was the past he didn't bother to acknowledge," she remarked.

"And his past reached out and changed my present and, I hope, my future," he said. "After I learned of Royce's existence a couple of years ago, I launched a search for him. I just wanted to get to know him, see if he needed anything. Because he was an FBI agent, he was pretty hard to find."

"But you found him eventually."

The words seemed to stick in Cort's throat before he said, "Not in time to meet him."

Niera couldn't help turning and letting her gaze lock with Cort's.

He continued. "One of my letters finally caught up with him. He wrote back that he was busy with an assignment in Honolulu and couldn't meet me right away. He said it would be best not to call, either, but we did correspond for a while. That's how I first learned about you."

She expressed surprise at that tidbit of information.

"Royce wrote about you in glowing terms," Cort continued. "In his last letter—the last one I received—he said he was falling in love with you."

Niera stared into the sand. "I'm not sure I want to hear this." She recovered after a moment. "Yes, I do. I want to know everything."

"I had to come to Honolulu on business. So I sent him a telegram giving him the name of my hotel, and

aid I hoped we could meet in the privacy of my room if
e got a chance. Actually, I arrived two days sooner
han I'd expected, but even so, I was two days too late."

"I'm sorry," she whispered. "But why did you do this
o me? I had nothing to do with his death."

His expression was as stricken as hers. "Don't you
hink I know that? I sensed from the moment we met
hat you were the terrific person Royce believed you to
e, and I was sure of it after I'd spent a couple of days
n your company. You can't believe I would have made
ove to you if I'd thought you'd killed my brother."

"So what was your game, exactly? You were at the
ospital here in Honolulu, weren't you? And at the airport in Los Angeles?"

"Yes," he admitted. "One of Royce's buddies in the
FBI office was keeping me informed about the case,
and about you. I knew you were being transferred,
and I was standing there on the hospital grounds that
last afternoon while you were on the lanai in your
wheelchair. I was trying to decide whether to speak
with you, and what to say, when suddenly you woke
up and saw me. I hadn't formed a precise plan, and I
panicked and left rather than talk to you. The next
day I had to fly back to Denver anyway, and I was
curious enough to take the same plane to Los Angeles
and be sure you actually were put on a connecting
flight to Billings."

"You were at the hospital earlier, too, weren't you?
Standing in the rain on the grounds outside my window
the day I regained full consciousness?"

He uttered a surprised yes, then added, "I didn't
know you saw me. And I thought you hadn't gotten a
close enough look at me that last afternoon at the hospital and at the L.A. airport to recognize me three months
later in Tahiti."

"Maybe I wouldn't have without my investigative experience."

"I wasn't sure exactly what I should do, but I knew I had to do something," he explained. "Were you a murderer or an angel? If you were guilty, I wanted to see you brought to justice. If you were innocent and I could help clear you, then I owed that to my brother, too, because he'd loved you.

"To start at the beginning," he continued, "the first time I saw you was right after I arrived in Honolulu. I read in the newspaper at the airport that Royce had been killed and that his partner was hospitalized. I knew that had to be you, although the newspaper didn't identify you."

"You sat in my room for a long time," she realized, "and you were wearing that special after shave."

"How could you know that?"

"It was a wisp in my subconscious."

"I talked to you, because talking to people in a coma is supposed to help them. But I never realized you were aware of my presence." He added wistfully, "You looked so beautiful, even then. And so vulnerable. Just sitting there with you, I understood why Royce loved you, and in a twisted way I envied him that. I'd been too caught up in my business to take time out to love anyone."

"Not emotionally available," she whispered.

"Not until I met you. Then I couldn't seem to stop my emotions from trampling my common sense."

He returned to his story. "I brought you a bird of paradise plant at the hospital. Somehow I couldn't take back the flowers even after Hal arrived. I only removed the card.

"Hal," he continued, "actually wasn't surprised to see me there. Though Royce had said he had no brothers or sisters, Hal had found my telegram, along with a letter Royce had started to write to me. When he checked Royce's security-clearance file later, he learned that we were mentioned, with the notation that Royce

d his mother had no contact with that side of the fam-
y."

"And Hal told you that I was a criminal suspect in
e case?"

"He showed me Royce's last letter, the unfinished
ne that I never received. He had written that he was
ry distressed and needed to confide in someone, but
at he didn't want to go to anyone in his department
t. He was uncovering evidence that the woman he
ved was in cahoots with the clothing counterfeiters."

"Was that the only evidence Hal had against me?"

"I don't think so, although they're not free with de-
ils, as I'm sure you know. I think there must have
en some other evidence, too—something that ap-
eared to be evidence against you, I mean."

"Well. Genuine phony evidence infiltrates the FBI.
teresting." After a pause, she prodded, "So you were
llowing me to see if Royce's suspicion was well
unded?"

"Sort of. All along, basic logic indicated that you
ouldn't have been injured yourself if you'd set the ex-
osives or known about them. But you were holding a
un when they found you unconscious, and you hadn't
ctually been with your partner per usual procedure. I
ad a burning urge to learn the truth about you, one way
r another. Now I'm not so sure that wasn't for my own
ake more than for my brother's."

"Royce's buddy in the Honolulu FBI office told you
'd be in Tahiti?"

"He apparently knew you'd be taking the cruise, but
ot that you'd be flying in ahead of time. When you
veren't on the ship that first day, I thought maybe you'd
ed to Hal and gone somewhere else, perhaps even
kipped the country for good. I was dumbfounded when
literally ran into you underwater off the coast of Bora
Bora. So once again, I ran away, in a manner of speak-
ng, until I could decide on the best way to approach

you. I didn't expect to see you again until dinner th
night. Encountering you at Bloody Mary's was a coinc
dence."

"I see," she murmured.

"If I seemed to run hot and cold, off and on, rig
after we met, it was because I was uncertain whether
could pull off even a minor charade. I didn't like lyir
to you, overtly or by omission," he said, "and I tried
pick my answers carefully. I fibbed about never havir
been in Hawaii because I was afraid you might r
member that you'd seen me on your last day in the ho
pital."

A raspberry-colored Frisbee arched over their head
and a dynamo of fur raced around their feet, then o
ward, chasing it.

"That dog reminds me of Ramby," she said. H
voice trailed off as she added, "You told me so muc
about yourself at first . . ."

"I thought talking about myself would encourage yo
to open up to me and talk about yourself." There was
long silence. "I slipped in a lot of details about my bus
ness operations and distribution network to make myse
look like a prime target, in case you really were marke
ing counterfeit designer clothing."

"You wanted to see if I'd make you an offer," sh
concluded for him.

"Instead, I wound up offering myself to you. No,
realize now that I kept rambling on about myself be
cause I wanted to share myself with you. And I wa
honestly planning to tell you all this after we got to you
apartment this afternoon. That's why I joined you i
Honolulu. But when I got here, I couldn't resist pro
longing what there was between us for one more night.
guess that's what I've been doing ever since I bega
falling for you that first day on Bora Bora—nurturin
and prolonging what was building between us, hopin

that you'd come to love me enough that my original
reasons for following you wouldn't matter."

She wanted to hang on to the love they had shared,
the love that had bloomed beneath the South Pacific sun
and renewed itself in the moonlight. "Everything you
told me since we met is true, except about never having
been in Hawaii before?"

Tenderly but firmly, he grasped her shoulders and
turned her around to face him. Then he released her.

"Cross my heart and hope to die." His gaze embraced her as his words spiraled warmth around her.
"And I think I will die inside, Niera, if you can't love
me anymore."

"You're not holding anything else back?"

"No." His assurance was emphatic.

"And you don't believe there's any possibility that
I'm a criminal conspirator?"

"Absolutely not."

She looked away, loving him. Furious with him, but
understanding his reasons for keeping secrets from her.

He misinterpreted her hesitation. "Niera, the FBI
doesn't really believe you were involved. You wouldn't
have been left free so long if they had incontrovertible
evidence against you."

"That's true. Unless they want me free here, hoping
that I'll lead them to my cohorts, since their investigation has fizzled out. Hal has informed me that I'm still
on vacation and I'm not to operate in an official capac-
ity. Also, I'm not to come into the office, so I won't
have access to all the technological resources and the
subsequent investigation files."

"I meant it last night when I said I was going to stay
here and help you solve this case."

She couldn't involve any civilian in a potentially
dangerous situation. She certainly wouldn't put Cort,
the man she loved, at risk.

"I don't want you here, Cort," she managed to say

coldly. "I'll be busy, and you'd just be in the way." She avoided his gaze. "I've got to go to my apartment right now, clean it up, and get resettled. We could meet for dinner later, before you go back to Denver. Unless you want to take an earlier flight."

His expression was stricken, but he insisted, "You're not getting rid of me that easily. I'll settle for dinner tonight, for any tidbit of attention you'll give me after the way I deceived you. But I won't be going back to Denver. I came here to be with you, to help you with this case."

"I can't accept assistance from a private citizen."

"You're not much more than that yourself," he reminded her. "Hal has told you that you have no official status at the moment." Seeing the different kind of pain that caused her, he quickly moved away from that subject. "Let's go to your apartment. I'll help you get settled. Then if you want me to stay in a hotel, I will."

"Okay," she relented. She could use some emotional support when she confronted that dinner setting for two: herself and a phantom.

She admitted to herself that she wanted one more night in Cort's arms before she talked him into returning to Denver. It was getting late in the day, and she wouldn't proceed with her private investigation until tomorrow, anyway.

They took a cab to her apartment.

She drew in a deep breath as she turned the key, then entered. The place didn't look bad, except for a layer of dust. But the scene appeared slightly warped, knick-knacks a bit askew, the candle holder off-center on the table, throw pillows in the wrong place.

All in all, the FBI had exercised restraint in searching her place—probably giving her credit for not being foolish enough to keep incriminating evidence there.

She preempted any polite remark on Cort's part.

"You don't have to say it's a nice place. I know it's ordinary. I rarely spend time here, except to sleep if I'm not away on assignment."

"It's tasteful and pleasant," he insisted. "We don't have much cleaning to do except maybe run the vacuum and wield a dust cloth." He crossed to the telephone. "I should call for reservations if there's a hotel nearby."

"You don't need to do that. Of course I want you to stay here." She added, "For tonight."

"Great, because this is the only place with a five-star rating as far as I'm concerned." He tossed that terrific double-dimpled smile over his shoulder as he carried their suitcases into the bedroom.

"Just hang your clothes in the closet," she told him.

As she walked to the table to remove the china and crystal, she heard the closet door sliding open in the bedroom.

"Where?" he called back. "There's not a spare millimeter of space in here."

She didn't recall her closet being overly crowded. "Use your masculine power to make some space." She carried the dishes to the kitchen sink.

She could hear the uneasiness in his next words, spoken scarcely loud enough for her to hear. "I thought you said you weren't into trendy clothes?"

She ambled to the bedroom door. "I'm not. Want to replenish my wardrobe from your private stock?"

"I don't think you need my help."

Poking her head through the door, she saw that he was examining a slinky silver disco dress. She'd been kidding about wanting him to choose her clothes, and this silver number definitely wasn't her style. "Why did you bring that with you?"

"I didn't." He turned to her, uncertainty in his eyes.

Then she saw the crammed closet behind him. She quickly crossed the room and pulled out one unfamiliar garment after another. Labels from virtually every expensive designer flashed before her eyes.

"Genuine phony stuff," she remarked eventually.

"I'd say not," Cort replied, his voice strangely tight. He'd been examining the labels, the fabrics, the workmanship. "These are the real things."

"Sure they are. The originals that counterfeiters make their copies from. This isn't bogus *merchandise*. It's bogus *evidence,* planted here to make me look guilty."

They discussed this for a while. Cort was a hundred percent on her side, incensed that someone had framed her. He concluded with "Besides, you're not so stupid as to keep incriminating evidence in your own apartment."

"Thanks. It's nice to know you have faith in my intelligence, if not my inherent honesty."

"The FBI didn't fall for it, or you would have been arrested."

"Unless they prefer to follow me instead," she reminded him. Angry and frustrated at the situation, she began unpacking her own suitcase, yanking drawers open, banging them closed.

"Wait a minute," Cort said, looking over her shoulder as she started to close her nightstand drawer. "Who's that?"

"Oh, Cort." She stepped back and slipped her free arm around his waist while lifting the photograph out of the drawer. "That's Royce."

A two-dimensional Royce stared up at them from a jungly green background. "I took that picture when we went hiking one Saturday on the Na Pali Coast on Kauai," she told Cort. "That was Royce's favorite part of Hawaii."

Cort's gaze was riveted to the photograph. Minutes ticked past while he studied it. He traced the outline of Royce's face with his fingertip.

Then the realization dawned on his features. "Is it my imagination, or—"

He strode to the mirror, looking back and forth from his own reflection to the image captured on film. He placed a blocking finger over Royce's mustache.

"Oh, God," Cort said finally. "Except for hair and eye color, we could almost be twins."

"Yes," Niera confirmed softly.

He didn't speak further, so she continued, "That's why, when I saw you in Honolulu and Los Angeles, and the first few days on the cruise, I thought Royce was still alive, in disguise for some reason. Having never seen Royce yourself, you couldn't have realized what an added torture that was for me."

"I knew it." His words were a whispered defeat. "I knew it as soon as I saw the resemblance between us in this photograph."

She misinterpreted his comments until he continued, "That's why you wouldn't stay with me, not in Tahiti, not even in Denver after you'd confirmed my true identity."

He turned back to her, his shoulders slumped, pure agony twisting his features.

"Cort—" She started toward him, opening her arms.

He drew himself upright and fixed her with a firm stare. "Will you forget all this and come back to Denver with me right now?"

"Cort, we went over all this less than two hours ago, and twice before that."

"I can assure you that Hal made it obvious that you're not a prime suspect in the case."

"Still, Cort," she declared in exasperation, "this is a puzzle that needs to be solved, unfinished business that has to be wound up."

"You have to find Royce's murderer?"

She hesitated before replying, "Yes."

"Because you loved Royce."

Shock glazed her features. "No!"

He ignored her protest. "Because you still love Royce."

"No!"

"All this time—on the *motu*, last night—I was just a stand-in. A surrogate lover. You were pretending that Royce was still alive."

"Cort, that's not true." She followed him, trying to put her arms around him as he reached for his suitcase.

"I guess you did want your own genuine phony after all," he said. "Well, I'm not willing to play that role."

"Cort, I never loved Royce." She fired the words at him, staccato, hoping they'd penetrate his emotional armor.

He pulled away from her and strode out of the bed-room.

"I love *you*." She had to shout those words to his retreating back.

He punctuated her statement with the slam of her front door.

Chapter 10

THREE DAYS.

At first she couldn't bring herself to believe that Cort didn't intend to return to her, didn't know beyond all doubt that it was only he whom she loved.

The bleak realization that she would never see him again gradually seeped into every cell of her being. It required all the willpower she could muster to continue with her clandestine investigation instead of curling up alone in her bed and crying twenty-four hours a day. She'd been telephoning Cort in Denver, but his office claimed he wasn't "available," and there was no answer at his home. Her nightly telephone calls to Megan provided little comfort, although she was grateful for a caring friend to talk to.

In some ways, she was more determined than ever to capture these criminals. This case had made Cort a vital part of her existence, then ripped him away from her.

Despite all her years of being happily alone, she suddenly couldn't envision a future without Cort.

Nip. That had been the older agents' nickname for her, because she'd always nipped at the heels of the bad guys until she'd herded them into a corral full of evidence. But now a black desolation was more than nipping at her—it was looming over her, threatening to swallow her up in its inescapable jaws.

For the moment, though, she was looking at the reflection of a man in the window of a coffee shop in the warehouse district. Her current tail, with his unattractive pink body, she decided, resembled a giant guinea pig minus fur. His bald head was sunburned, his chubby pink legs stuffed their way out of his Bermuda shorts, and his thick forearms were visible beneath the short sleeves of his phosphorescent orange aloha-print shirt. His Hawaiian attire was actually more appropriate for blending with the crowd in Honolulu than a conservative business suit would have been, but it certainly did look silly on him.

Niera had been followed for the past three days and had grown used to the routine, but this agent was even more incompetent than the others. She wondered briefly where Hal could have found these men. She knew he was importing them from other cities, since she would immediately have recognized the Honolulu operatives, but these men didn't seem to know the first thing about how a good agent ran a tail.

Thinking of the incompetent agents made her ask herself what kind of imbeciles had been assigned to this case after the explosion. Whoever they were, they had found no new leads and had let the investigation peter out. Why? Niera wondered. Now, more than three months later, she was finding plenty of leads, and they were paying off so well that she expected to solve the case soon.

In fact, she intended to buy a gun and close in on the

criminals within the next few days. She was familiar with the back streets of Honolulu, where one could purchase firearms quickly, cheaply, and secretly. She'd left her own FBI-issue revolver at the branch office in Los Angeles, since she couldn't take it to Tahiti, and she hadn't retrieved it. She knew Hal wouldn't issue her another after forbidding her to pursue this case.

It took her only a few minutes to lose her tail, and she immediately began to follow him instead. She would delight in tailing him straight into Hal's office and telling the boss how this imported agent had messed up.

He stopped often to wipe his perspiring face on his shirtsleeves, but seemed never to have the slightest clue that he was being stalked.

A growing uneasiness pervaded her as the agent led her deeper into the warehouse district. It was closing time for most businesses, and employees hurrying along the sidewalks provided some cover for her. Yet she knew the area soon would be so deserted that she wouldn't be able to keep him in sight without being spotted herself.

The number of people thinned as dusk filtered down, transforming the innocuous mammoth warehouses into hungry, hulking dinosaurs.

Niera knew she couldn't remain inconspicuous much longer. And she also suspected that the tall pink guinea pig was smarter than he looked and might be baiting her into a trap.

She had begun to seek intermittent cover in doorways when at last he stopped, opened the side door of a warehouse farther down the street, and disappeared inside.

She waited more than half an hour, then surreptitiously circled the warehouse.

Should she follow him in there or not? Caution told her not to, but a strong hunch urged her on.

There was no pay telephone nearby, and neighboring

buildings were locked and deserted, so she couldn't call for backup. She returned to a small window she'd found in the back of the warehouse. The opening was tiny, like her. A larger person couldn't have shimmied through.

Darkness gaped before her. Then she was inside. As her eyes adjusted, she saw that a dim bulb burned over one area in the center, and she heard a low hum of voices. Glancing around, she saw a ladder leading to a loft. She climbed it, then inched her way toward the light.

"I don't see no reason to keep tailin' her, anyway." A whiny voice reached her ears.

"I think you're right, Duane," another man's voice agreed. "It's time to wrap this up, one way or another."

She reached a point where she could peek around a barricade of boxes at the scene below. A distinguished-looking man with silver sideburns, wearing a three-piece suit, was speaking. So the other man, the tall guinea pig, must be Duane. A buxom young woman with strawberry-blond hair completed the trio.

"So what do ya think we oughta do? Clyde? Evelyn?" Duane asked, stepping aside. Until then, Niera hadn't been able to see a third man, who was seated.

With shock, she recognized him and clenched her fist against her mouth, a self-imposed gag against crying out, then swallowed back the bitterness that rose in her throat.

Cort!

Her heart dropped so far and so hard that she thought it might tumble down around their feet.

Then she realized her heart was in place, but its loud thundering must surely be revealing her presence.

The man she loved, the man she had trusted, was seated in that chair among the other criminals. Evidently Cort was using his legitimate business as a front for the distribution of counterfeit clothing. The thin light from the bulb glared off his blond hair.

Clyde approached him and leaned toward his face. "We're not normally violent people, but we've had it with your lies. You're not gonna get away with ripping us off. There would have been enough bucks for all of us. This is your last chance. Tell us what you did with the shipment, Royce."

Royce! Niera strained, trying to get a better look at his face.

"I keep telling you I'm not Royce."

Joyful relief mingled with a rising panic. She could see now that Cort's arms were stretched back behind the chair; probably his wrists were tied. Niera was thrilled to learn that Cort wasn't a criminal, but she was terrified to see him in such danger. No wonder he hadn't contacted her in the last three days!

Her mind chased possibilities for action while she listened to the conversation below. Cort repeated his explanations about being Royce's brother. The others, who obviously didn't believe him, simply increased their threats.

Earlier, as she'd crept toward the edge of the loft, her hand had slipped into the open top of a box. An instant's excitement had flicked through her when she felt the barrel of a gun, but chemical fumes from molded plastic had assailed her nostrils at the same time, and she had realized with dismay that it was a toy weapon.

She eased back that way, found the carton, and removed a plastic machine gun.

Thank goodness for little boys who wanted to be Sylvester Stallone, she thought. And wasn't it wonderful that crooks who imported counterfeit clothing also imported cheap toys?

She couldn't see details of the toy in the darkness. She hoped it was a credible replica of a machine gun.

"You shouldn't have stuck with that little blonde," Clyde was saying as she sneaked back to the edge of the loft. "If you'd stayed away from Honolulu, we'd have believed you were killed in that explosion. Lucky Duane spotted you coming out of her apartment and had the good sense to snatch you and hold you until I got back."

Clyde circled Cort's chair, continuing, "Funny thing is, it was your girl friend the Van Drexels were following on the ship. They'd never met you, Royce, so they wouldn't have recognized you even without the bleach job. They reported she was meeting with some clothing distributor to sell the merchandise through him. We hadn't checked that out yet, since I just got back."

Niera slithered to the edge of the loft above them, lying flat so they wouldn't have much of a target. She held the fake machine gun so it would catch only a tiny shaft of light.

"What're we gonna do with him?" Duane asked Clyde. "Dump him off the boat or pack him up and ship him back to Taiwan?"

"Hands up!" Niera yelled.

They all looked up and around as Niera shouted, *"Now!"* Evelyn caught a glimpse of her and threw her skinny arms straight up. Clyde followed his girl friend's cue, but Duane started to reach under his shirt.

"Don't even think about it!" Niera treated him to her best make-my-day shout.

Finally, Duane put his hands up, too.

Before they had time to wonder why she didn't stand up, she ordered Evelyn to untie Cort.

The instant his hands were free, Cort sprang out of the chair and seized the pistol from the waistband of Duane's Bermuda shorts. Cort then supervised Evelyn as she securely tied up Clyde and Duane.

Only then did Niera make her way down to the main floor, still carrying her plastic weapon.

"Damn!" Clyde exclaimed. "All she had was one of those damned toys!"

"Congratulations," she told him. "Your fakes look authentic."

She took Duane's pistol from Cort. He tied Evelyn's wrists together, then found a telephone and called the police.

Niera spent the next few days convincing Cort—very thoroughly—that she'd never loved Royce—but that didn't mean she and Cort could put Royce completely out of their thoughts.

She reached for Cort's hand and gave it a squeeze. "You do understand that we can't force Royce to see you or talk to you as long as he refuses?"

"That's fine with me," Cort said quietly. "Happily-ever-after may be in store for you and me, but this was no fairy tale. I suppose I ought to be forgiving and gen-erous, ready to offer my emotional and financial support to my poor, disadvantaged older brother, but that's not going to happen, at least not any time soon. I can't forgive him for what he tried to do to you."

She said good-bye to Cort and drove to the Honolulu office of the FBI, where she found Royce himself sitting across the desk from Hal Symons.

"You were right, as usual," Hal said without pream-ble. "We found Royce living near the Na Pali Coast on Kauai, where you advised us to look."

She and Royce stared at each other, his ice-blue eyes versus her stormy gray ones. He really did resemble the man she loved, Niera thought, but no way had he ever been Mr. Right.

Royce sneezed, grabbing a tissue off Hal's desk. He said between sniffles, "I guess I don't have to worry about spoiling my romantic image anymore."

"Your image couldn't possibly get any more spoiled," she said. "The only thing I haven't figured out is why you bothered to do all that romancing."

"Same as any guy with a pretty blonde. I was a
tracted to you."

"And he probably assumed," Hal interjected gruffl
"that he was so irresistible he could distract you fro
the case." He turned to Royce. "Surprise, pal. *She's*
pro."

"So that was the point of telling me right before th
explosion that you loved me, to distract me from cor
tinuing with the case after your supposed death, becaus
of grief or guilt, or whatever?"

Royce glanced away, flicking his cigarette ash int
the brass tray. "Sure."

Hal had already told Niera that Royce would be of
fered immunity in exchange for his testimony agains
the others, so she knew he had no reason not to tell all
Duane, Clyde, and company had been charged with
half-dozen felonies, including kidnapping Cort, s
Royce's testimony against them would be crucial. Also
the authorities were always reluctant to send former
law-enforcement officers to prison because of th
danger they might face at the hands of the other con
victs.

There was a pause before Royce added, "You wer
closing in too fast, Niera, forcing my hand. I thought
was covered, but you were putting the pieces togethe
too quick. I needed time to market the merchandise."

Royce took another long drag on the cigarette. "The
I got the telegram from my dear long-lost brother." H
laughed bitterly. "How swell of him to finally seek m
out. One of the first things I did after I became an FB
agent was track down my father. Imagine my surpris
when I found that the man who'd abandoned me wa
raising and caring for three stepdaughters as if they wer
his own. A regular family man."

He continued, "I never contacted dear old Dad o
anyone else on that side of the family. But I'd notice
that my younger half brother looked enough like me t

e a twin, except for the color of his hair and eyes. I
ept an eye on him, so I knew all about his business.
mpersonating him, dealing with his business asso-
iates, was going to be my ticket to sure profits in dis-
ibuting bogus designer label clothes."

"And if it ran him out of business, so what?"

"Exactly. Then he could struggle like I had to."

"So you didn't want Cort to show up here and dis-
over the resemblance, and you were careful not to let
eople know you even had a brother?"

"His trip to Hawaii forced me to speed up my time-
able—that and the fact that you were closing in. I orig-
nally infiltrated the gang on the Mainland, planning to
ather enough evidence to hotdog my way into a major
ust of the whole ring. But when I saw that the bucks
ould be better than the bust, I finagled a temporary
ransfer to Honolulu on the pretext of following through
n the case. Of course I was really covering for them
ere until I could take my profit. And what I did wasn't
ll that bad, when you think about it. Who's hurt, really,
y some cheap clothes? That's what most of us wear all
he time."

"You'd always planned on cutting out Clyde and the
thers?" she asked.

Royce shrugged. "Not always. But we all know
here's no honor among thieves. I didn't intend to stay
n the counterfeit-merchandise smuggling business. I
ould have made a fortune on that one shipment, and
vho were they going to tell?"

"You moved all the merchandise out of the ware-
ouse on the pier before you blew it up?"

Royce nodded. "Moved it to Kauai the night before,
vith a little help from some unquestioning seamen.
Then I set the explosives to be detonated later. Clyde,
Evelyn, and the Van Drexels were on another buying
rip to the Orient, and Duane spent most of his time
getting pickled in the local bars. I left enough merchan-

dise in the warehouse to provide believable flotsam
Royce's voice caught for the first time. "I didn't inten
for you to be hurt, Niera."

"Of course not," she responded sardonically.

"You wouldn't have been physically injured," h
persisted, as if there were no other way of being hur
"if you'd stayed in the car like I ordered you to."

"I had some silly idea about protecting my partner."

"In a way, so did I. When the moon came out for
moment, I saw you at the landward end of the pie
moving toward the warehouse. That's why I set off th
explosives ahead of schedule. I dived into the wate
right away, grabbed the scuba equipment I had strappe
to a piling underneath, and headed for the detonatin
mechanism, which I'd attached to another piling. I too
a chance of being hurt myself by detonating the exple
sion as soon as I did, before you'd be close enough
be killed."

"You're one swell fellow," she said sarcasticall
"Besides taking the risk of killing me, you plante
phony evidence against me in your desk, just enough t
make it look as if you were hesitant to inform on m
until you had incontrovertible proof. You backed that u
with an unfinished letter to Cort saying that you sus
pected me but couldn't bring yourself to turn me in
And of course, you knew that the subsequent investiga
tion would reveal complicity on the part of an FBI age
in concealing evidence and setting false trails. The in
vestigators couldn't know that agent had been you rathe
than me. None of my leads panned out for subseque
investigators, because you'd altered my reports."

"Uh-huh." Royce nodded, displaying not one whit
remorse.

"And as further insurance, you'd told that gang
felons that I was in on the scam with you. You kne
they'd turn me in if they were caught, and you als

knew they'd concentrate on watching me rather than searching for you."

"Nice touch, I thought."

"By the way," she said, "thanks for the new wardrobe of designer originals. Now the evidence room has a touch of class."

"I knew I could easily plant those in your apartment while you were investigating the explosion and doing all the paperwork. I was gambling that the other agents would find my letter to Cort and search your place before you got home."

"And my being taken to the hospital was an extra plus." She bit off the words.

Hal was called out of the office for a moment.

Royce fumbled in his pocket for another cigarette. "Was there ever any possibility," he asked Niera without looking at her, "that you might have chucked it all and thrown in with me, come to Brazil or wherever?"

"No chance, not ever."

"That's what I figured."

Hal returned, and they discussed other details of the case. Finally, Niera was ready to leave.

As she turned toward the door, Royce made a weak attempt at a joke. "At least you didn't use that old line on me: 'I always get my man.'"

"But I do always get my man," she reminded him, allowing her lips to quirk with the hint of a satisfied smile. "In fact, this time I got two—and both in the right way."

Professionally, she'd gotten the man she'd be glad to be rid of. And personally, she'd gotten the man she intended never to release, singlehandedly planning to give him a lifetime sentence, with no parole.

Quietly, she closed the door on the past and hurried toward her future.

*   *   *

"You're being shanghaied," she told Cort as she parked her car at the marina.

"Slow boat to China?"

"Fast boat to Molokai."

She'd filled him in on all the details of the case as soon as she'd returned from Hal's office yesterday.

"Molokai," she explained, aiming the speedboat she'd borrowed from Hal in that direction, "is the least developed major island." She smiled a promise at him. "There are lots of isolated coves where we can pretend we're back on the *motu* in Tahiti. Well, almost."

"You brought a large supply of food?" he asked.

"Got to keep your strength up."

"Champagne?"

"Yep. And a special treat, Dr Pepper."

"Too bad," he said, "that we're wearing American-style clothes instead of *pareos*."

"We can change. I brought two along."

A short while later, they pulled the boat onto a deserted crescent of golden sand on Molokai. Wading the last few feet in to shore, Niera remarked, "You were right. These waves have followed us from Tahiti. I recognize every one of them."

"The water isn't as clear here." Cort's gaze caressed her. "But everything else is sure a lot clearer now."

"Including the fact that I love you," she emphasized.

"And that I love you." He gathered her into his arms and kissed her deeply.

An onrushing wave almost knocked them off their feet, urging them forward.

"Let's fairly share the unloading of the boat," she said. "I'll carry the *pareos* and you carry everything else."

"Speaking of *pareos*, I've been thinking how great you'd look in a *pareo* of white lace, with a long train . . . An old Polynesian style in a new design."

"I see," she mused aloud. "As in something old, something new."

"And you'll need something borrowed," he said. "I could give you all my love with no strings attached, but I'd rather make you pay it back, with interest, for a lifetime."

"Those terms seem reasonable."

Cort reached for her hand, but she slipped it into the pocket of her peach-colored shorts. He watched her intently, a slight anxiety edging into his voice as he delivered his summation. "So what we're working up to here is something old, something new, something borrowed, and—"

"Something black," she interrupted, pulling her closed hand out of her pocket, then slowly opening it to reveal the black pearl nestled in her palm, in its new gold setting. In a ring.

"Doesn't rhyme." His fingertips stroked her palm as he scooped up the ring. He caressed her third finger, left hand, then slipped the ring onto its permanent home.

"Then we'll just make up our own poetry from now on."

"I suspect we can do a pretty good job of that." Drawing her into his arms, he brushed his lips across hers.

They reveled in just holding each other for several minutes, their bodies pressed lightly together.

"I'm told I can get a transfer to the Denver FBI office whenever I want to," Niera said. "Promise to keep me warm in the winter?"

"Absolutely. Or Dressed for Excess can open a branch in Honolulu. I've gotten pretty attached to the tropics. We'll work out the details."

Her gaze meandered lovingly across his features as she tilted her face for his kiss. "Just so I can keep you under close scrutiny for the rest of our lives."

SECOND CHANCE AT LOVE

Be Sure to Read These New Releases!

PRINCE CHARMING REPLIES #430
by Sherryl Woods

After advertising for Prince Charming
in the local Personals, Katie Stewart doesn't
lack for suitors. Her new admirers
arouse the jealousy—and ardor—of her
handsome, dynamic boss, Ross Chandler.
Suddenly, Katie's life is ever-so-romantic—
both on the job and after hours!

DESIRE'S DESTINY #431
by Jamisan Whitney

Truck driver/philosopher Freddy Rotini
is challenged to the hilt by his new role as
wagonmaster, and by one of the tourists
he leads along the Oregon trail, lovely
Johanna Remington. The wagon train
becomes a comedy of errors—and the
romance a drama of blazing passion.

Please send the titles I've checked above. Mail orders to:

BERKLEY PUBLISHING GROUP
390 Murray Hill Pkwy., Dept. B
East Rutherford, NJ 07073

POSTAGE & HANDLING:
$1.00 for one book, $.25 for each
additional. Do not exceed $3.50.

NAME _____

ADDRESS _____

CITY _____

STATE _____ ZIP _____

Please allow 6 weeks for delivery.
Prices are subject to change without notice.

BOOK TOTAL $_____

SHIPPING & HANDLING $_____

APPLICABLE SALES TAX $_____
(CA, NJ, NY, PA)

TOTAL AMOUNT DUE $_____
PAYABLE IN US FUNDS.
(No cash orders accepted.)

SECOND CHANCE AT LOVE

COMING NEXT MONTH

SURRENDER THE DAWN #434
by Jan Mathews

Undercover detective Laura Davis
was raped on a sting operation headed by
federal agent Kyle Patterson, who vows
to help her vanquish the memories.
The saying "love conquers all" is put
to the test...and triumphs.

A WARM DECEMBER #435
by Jacqueline Topaz

When her sister goads her about her
lack of marital prospects, Merrie McGregor
invents an engagement between herself
and eligible bachelor Dave Anders. Not only
does Dave agree to be her fictitious fiancé—
he also wants to be her real husband!

SECOND CHANCE AT LOVE

___ 0-425-09745-5	CUPID'S VERDICT #386 Jackie Leigh	$2.25
___ 0-425-09746-3	CHANGE OF HEART #387 Helen Carter	$2.25
___ 0-425-09831-1	PLACES IN THE HEART #388 Delaney Devers	$2.25
___ 0-425-09832-X	A DASH OF SPICE #389 Kerry Price	$2.25
___ 0-425-09833-8	TENDER LOVING CARE #390 Jeanne Grant	$2.25
___ 0-425-09834-6	MOONSHINE AND MADNESS #391 Kate Gilbert	$2.25
___ 0-425-09835-4	MADE FOR EACH OTHER #392 Aimee Duvall	$2.25
___ 0-425-09836-2	COUNTRY DREAMING #393 Samantha Quinn	$2.25
___ 0-425-09943-1	NO HOLDS BARRED #394 Jackie Leigh	$2.25
___ 0-425-09944-X	DEVIN'S PROMISE #395 Kelly Adams	$2.25
___ 0-425-09945-8	FOR LOVE OF CHRISTY #396 Jasmine Craig	$2.25
___ 0-425-09946-6	WHISTLING DIXIE #397 Adrienne Edwards	$2.25
___ 0-425-09947-4	BEST INTENTIONS #398 Sherryl Woods	$2.25
___ 0-425-09948-2	NIGHT MOVES #399 Jean Kent	$2.25
___ 0-425-10048-0	IN NAME ONLY #400 Mary Modean	$2.25
___ 0-425-10049-9	RECLAIM THE DREAM #401 Liz Grady	$2.25
___ 0-425-10050-2	CAROLINA MOON #402 Joan Darling	$2.25
___ 0-425-10051-0	THE WEDDING BELLE #403 Diana Morgan	$2.25
___ 0-425-10052-9	COURTING TROUBLE #404 Laine Allen	$2.25
___ 0-425-10053-7	EVERYBODY'S HERO #405 Jan Mathews	$2.25
___ 0-425-10080-4	CONSPIRACY OF HEARTS #406 Pat Dalton	$2.25
___ 0-425-10081-2	HEAT WAVE #407 Lee Williams	$2.25
___ 0-425-10082-0	TEMPORARY ANGEL #408 Courtney Ryan	$2.25
___ 0-425-10083-9	HERO AT LARGE #409 Steffie Hall	$2.25
___ 0-425-10084-7	CHASING RAINBOWS #410 Carole Buck	$2.25
___ 0-425-10085-5	PRIMITIVE GLORY #411 Cass McAndrew	$2.25
___ 0-425-10225-4	TWO'S COMPANY #412 Sherryl Woods	$2.25
___ 0-425-10226-2	WINTER FLAME #413 Kelly Adams	$2.25
___ 0-425-10227-0	A SWEET TALKIN' MAN #414 Jackie Leigh	$2.25
___ 0-425-10228-9	TOUCH OF MIDNIGHT #415 Kerry Price	$2.25
___ 0-425-10229-7	HART'S DESIRE #416 Linda Raye	$2.25
___ 0-425-10230-0	A FAMILY AFFAIR #417 Cindy Victor	$2.25
___ 0-425-10513-X	CUPID'S CAMPAIGN #418 Kate Gilbert	$2.50
___ 0-425-10514-8	GAMBLER'S LADY #419 Cait Logan	$2.50
___ 0-425-10515-6	ACCENT ON DESIRE #420 Christa Merlin	$2.50
___ 0-425-10516-4	YOUNG AT HEART #421 Jackie Leigh	$2.50

Available at your local bookstore or return this form to:

SECOND CHANCE AT LOVE
THE BERKLEY PUBLISHING GROUP, Dept. B
390 Murray Hill Parkway, East Rutherford, NJ 07073

Please send me the titles checked above. I enclose _____. Include $1.00 for postage and handling if one book is ordered; add 25¢ per book for two or more not to exceed $3.50 CA, NJ, NY and PA residents please add sales tax. Prices subject to change without notice and may be higher in Canada. Do not send cash.

NAME _____

ADDRESS _____

CITY _____ STATE/ZIP _____

(Allow six weeks for delivery.)

Sweeping Stories of Captivating Romance

☐ 0-441-58639-2	**NOT SO WILD A DREAM** Francine Rivers	$3.95
☐ 0-441-64449-X	**OUTLAW'S EMBRACE** Francine Rivers	$3.95
☐ 0-441-80926-X	**TEXAS LILY** Stephanie Blake	$3.95
☐ 0-441-58679-1	**ONE FERVENT FIRE** Karen Harper	$3.95
☐ 0-441-02146-8	**A FIRE IN THE HEART** Karen Harper	3.95
☐ 0-441-51574-6	**FOREVER THE FLAME** Nora Hess	$3.95
☐ 0-441-62860-5	**ONDINE** Shannon Drake	$4.50
☐ 0-515-09260-6	**AURORA** Kathryn Atwood	$3.95
☐ 0-441-80221-4	**THE TENDER DEVIL** Colleen Shannon	$3.95
☐ 0-441-05384-X	**SAVAGE SURRENDER** Cassie Edwards	$3.95
☐ 0-441-75348-5	**SANDENNY** Maryhelen Clague	$3.95

Please send the titles I've checked above. Mail orders to:

BERKLEY PUBLISHING GROUP
390 Murray Hill Pkwy., Dept. B
East Rutherford, NJ 07073

POSTAGE & HANDLING:
$1.00 for one book, $.25 for each
additional. Do not exceed $3.50.

NAME _____

ADDRESS _____

CITY _____

STATE _____ ZIP _____

Please allow 6 weeks for delivery.
Prices are subject to change without notice.

BOOK TOTAL	$_____
SHIPPING & HANDLING	$_____
APPLICABLE SALES TAX (CA, NJ, NY, PA)	$_____
TOTAL AMOUNT DUE PAYABLE IN US FUNDS. (No cash orders accepted.)	$_____